THE
OUTCAST

CLAIMED BY THE RED HAND 1

ORC

THE OUTCAST

CLAIMED BY THE RED HAND 1

ORC

JORDAN CASTILLO PRICE

jCPBOOKS.com

Print edition published in the
United States in 2025 by JCP Books
www.jcpbooks.com

First Print Edition

ISBN-978-1-944779-43-6

Names and Places

NAMES

Quinn - horseman from The Fortifications
Bess - slave from The Fortifications
Archie - slave from the territories
Marok - orc general
Borkul - orc warrior
Akala - Marok's late wife, Borkul's sister
Taruut - orc shaman
Ul-Rott - orc chieftain
Destroyer - warhorse

PLACES

Fortifications - massive walled city surrounded by wild territories
Wasteland - large stretch of barren land beyond the territories
Red Hand Clan - Marok's clan of orcs
Two Swords Clan - warring clan from across the river

1

QUINN

Five silver pieces. Four for my horse, and one for my saddle. Such small coins—but they carried the weight of everything I'd lost.

I watched the buyer lead Mercy away. My steady gray mare was worth at least double what I'd settled for. Any horseman worth his salt could see her value, but considering the scandal that now followed me through the Fortifications, I was lucky to find a buyer at all.

I only hoped it would be enough to pay for my passage out of the damned place.

As I spotted a busy courier shop on my way to the city gates, I wondered if the owner might've given me a better deal. But I was well aware of how their mounts were treated, and I wouldn't have trusted poor Mercy to their care for any price. I'd been strict with her these past few years, but never cruel. How could I bear the thought of some careless rider digging his heels into her flanks, or hauling on her bit with heavy hands?

Or worse, beating a few more miles out of her.

Early on, I'd figured out that a whip was best used sparingly, and never in anger. Especially with the young colts who hadn't learned to mind their feet.

I'd taught Mercy well. I trusted she would remember her training...whether her next master deserved it or not.

Still, the thought gnawed at me. Maybe I shouldn't have given her up. But conditions were rough outside the Fortifications' walls, and Mercy was used to soft stabling and sweet hay. She wasn't cut out for life on the road.

Then again, I probably wasn't either. In the city, I had my hot meals at the tavern, regular warm baths at the public houses, and a proper bed. Out there, I'd be lucky to find shelter in a barn. But thanks to one reckless moment of weakness, there wasn't a single noble house that would hire me.

I'd have to take my chances beyond the walls. Out there, in the territories between the Fortifications and the Wasteland, the roads were wild and the towns were wilder—but at least a man wouldn't be judged by his secrets, only his skills. That was the more important currency.

But first, I had to get there. And for that, I needed money.

I clutched the five coins as I made my way to the caravan, and the metal bit into my palm. Was it too late to change my mind? I could still shove the damned payment back into the buyer's hand and grab Mercy by the reins—

A vendor who always used to flash me a friendly smile now avoided my gaze as her eyes darted away like a guilty child's. Another turned his back, muttering under his breath.

The Fortifications were huge...but even so, news traveled fast.

There was no future for me here.

Soon enough, I reached the broad stone wall that gave the Fortifications its name. A scattering of crows perched on top had their beady black eyes on me as I strode out through the gate. I'm not tied down anymore, I told myself. I'm free.

I didn't feel free, though. I felt empty.

The caravan had gathered a short walk from the heavy iron gates. Close enough to hear the guards calling out challenges, far enough that its stores were safe from the quick-fingered beggars working the gate. The caravan belonged to Northern wool merchants, no-nonsense people who kept to themselves, from a province where sheep outnumbered men ten to one. While they might not be much for chitchat, their elaborate carpets sold for a good price in the Fortifications.

Business had been good. Their wagons were packed with city-made things—forged metals and blown glass—to take back north. Good for them, but not for me. With cargo taking up all that room, passage wouldn't come cheap.

But I wouldn't last a day in the lawless territory on my own, especially without a horse.

I caught a gate guard looking me up and down with his lip curled and hate in his eyes, and I knew that even if it took every last coin, getting far, far away would be worth it. I had thoroughly sold myself on the idea of a fresh start when I rounded a wagon and saw a pair of men having a heated discussion beside the rig's team. One horse, a chestnut mare, stood with her weight off her left leg.

The older man was grizzled and ropy, and he'd clearly

made this journey before. He shook his head and said, "This isn't just costing us gold. It's wasting time."

"I swear the horse was sound when I bought it." The younger one's voice broke. He was barely old enough to shave.

"And this is how you learn that the Fortifications are a filthy place where every seller will do his damnedest to take advantage of you."

"I was careful!"

With a weary sigh, the older man unsheathed a long, sturdy blade and held it out hilt-first to the youth. "The nag had better be ready for tonight's stew pot by the time I find a replacement."

"Wait," I said—and they both turned in surprise. Everyone knows you don't contradict a Northerner. They're a stubborn bunch—and they don't take kindly to outsiders telling them what to do. "Mind if I have a look?"

The boy looked hopeful, but the older one scowled harder.

I said, "I'm as invested as you are in putting the Fortifications behind us. What have you got to lose?"

The older one sized me up. I knew what he saw: a city man, slim and clean-shaven, with long, dark hair glossy from the baths and clothes too fine for honest work. But my sure stance and callused hands marked me as someone who knew his way around horses.

The man gave a brief grunt—as close to a *yes* as I'd get from a Northerner. The younger one hung back, eying me warily as I stepped up to examine the mare.

I crouched and ran my hands up and down each leg, checking for any heat or swelling in the joints. Her hide was caked in dust, but otherwise felt strong and healthy under my sure hands—until I reached her left forehoof. A pebble had lodged beneath the horseshoe, nestled just between the frog and heel. "Go get the farrier," I told the young man. "He'll have the caravan up and running in no time. Unless your heart is set on horse stew."

I was well acquainted with the farrier...and I made sure to busy myself on the far side of the caravan when he arrived. I'd always liked the man's sense of humor. And I was in no mood for the look of disgust that would surely be in his eyes.

My reputation lay in ashes, and I'd struck the match myself. A dozen years I'd spent building my good name, only to have it all dashed by one regretful slip. I'm not talking about the things I got up to with the apprentice blacksmith, either. He and I had done the deed several times before with no one any the wiser. It had been easy enough to catch his eye—that sort of thing usually was. But after the last time we'd shared a bed—during the afterglow, with wine in my belly and an overblown sense of affinity—I'd made the big mistake of leaning in for a kiss.

He'd stormed out in a rage, spewing ugly words. The next morning, my position in a wealthy merchant's stables had been filled by someone else. And every house that had made me an offer before was no longer interested in my services.

Evidently, getting off with another man could be overlooked. But heaven forbid you show them a bit of affection.

At least horses still made sense to me, even if nothing else did. And the Northerners recognized useful skills when they saw them—they offered me passage and let me keep one of my precious coins besides.

The caravan lurched into motion. The crows at the gate scattered as I set off toward my new life, more or less convinced I was eager to see what fortune the future had in store.

Arrin, the younger man, had saved a seat for me on his wagon—and over the course of the next week, we kept each other company. At first he didn't say much, but after a day or two of staring off down the road together, a few words were exchanged, and then entire conversations.

When I caught the way he looked at me when he thought I wasn't watching—that familiar mix of interest and hesitation—I even suspected he'd like to be more than just friends. But I didn't encourage him to swap anything but stories. He was green as spring grass, all wide-eyed wonder at the world beyond his village.

I wasn't about to jeopardize my place in the caravan. Besides, I knew what I liked in a man, and earnest young shepherds didn't stir my blood. I preferred the big, burly type, rough-hewn and strong-handed.

The sort who wanted nothing to do with love.

At least Arrin's rambling was a decent distraction from the tedium of the journey. Once the excitement of being outside the Fortifications' walls wore off, a certain sameness set in. The endless bump and grind of the wagon wheels, the creak of overhead branches swaying in the wind, and the ever-present birdsong....

Which, I'd realized, had gone suddenly quiet—just as a crossbow bolt shrieked past, nicking my ear, to lodge in Arrin's throat. His eyes didn't even have a chance to widen before he toppled off the wagon bench and was crushed beneath the churning wheels.

"No," I gasped, reaching for him—though it was already too late. My stomach lurched as the wheels did their work, and bile burned in my throat.

He was just a boy. And now he'd never be a man.

"Don't kill 'em *all* off, ya dumbfuck," a harsh voice called out. "Save some for the slavers!"

I launched myself off the wagon, landing on my feet with my hand on my whip. I mostly used it to keep spooked horses from stamping on my toes, but years of practice had made that whip an extension of my will. It never missed its target.

Raiders streamed from a gap in the trees. A whip might not seem like much protection against a sword, but it's got a much longer reach. My first swing struck true, and a raider's sword went flying into the undergrowth.

I whirled around and scanned for my next target. There were a good half dozen raiders, but between the Northerners and the mercenaries, we could handle them. My whip cracked, striking a scarred raider on the forearm. He cursed and reeled back, but didn't drop his sword—a long, vicious blade that was obviously well-used.

One of our mercenaries spotted me facing off with the swordsman and hurried over to help. The man hadn't been much of a traveling companion. Dull as dirt, with a habit of stating the obvious, starting each day by complaining about the weather. But two against one were odds I'd take any time.

My adversary's grin should have warned me. No man smiles when he's outmatched. I heard something whoosh through the air at my back, but by then it was too late. Our mercenary had chosen his side...and it wasn't mine.

His club caught me at the base of my skull, and my world went black.

2

QUINN

Two weeks later....

The slave trader burst into the tent with a flourish of his tattered silk robes. "Look lively, crew. A buyer caravan is on its way—and their coffers are busting with gold!"

As if his guards needed any more reason to poke at us. At least a dozen unfortunates—including me—had been dragged through the territories and dumped off in the middle of the Wasteland with nothing to do but sit in our cages and dread whatever fate had in store for us next. Meanwhile, the guards had nothing to do but antagonize us. I couldn't say what was worse—being sold, or not being sold. Rumor had it that anyone left after the day's trading could be had for a pittance...little enough that the guards could pool their money and take the unsold goods off their employer's hands.

And that once they were through with the unlucky slave,

there'd be one less mouth left to feed.

Generally, it was just the women who had to worry about the guards buying them. But there are exceptions to every rule.

A thick brute of a guard with a face like a diseased bull testicle paused to peer between the bars of my cage with a lingering look. I'd made fast enemies with him my first day here by shouting at him to stop his horse-whipping.

No one likes being told they're wrong—least of all by someone in chains.

But I couldn't stop myself.

The guard leaned toward the bars, just out of reach, and pitched his voice low and mean. "Caravan's coming. You think them's people on it? Hah. Guess again. Way out here in the Wasteland, you never know what kind of beast will show up."

I ignored him.

"Ya hear me, you stuck-up git? I said, they ain't people."

I wasn't about to rise to his bait, but the sheepish woman in the cage beside me let her curiosity get the best of her. "What do you mean, they're not people?"

Bollocks smiled. A grim, ugly thing. And though he answered her, he kept his flinty little eyes on me. "Oh, they walk on two legs just like you and me, and they got coin to spend...but no sir, they ain't people."

There was hardly enough room in my cage to turn around, so I lounged against the back and looked up at the top as if the bars were the most fascinating thing in the world.

My fellow prisoner didn't follow my lead. "What are they?" she asked, horrified.

Bollocks wet his lips eagerly and lowered his voice. "I'll

bet you that caravan's full of orcs."

"There's no such thing," the woman snapped—though the tone in her voice conveyed she wasn't entirely convinced.

"That's what I used to think," Bollocks claimed. "That's what anyone living inside the safe walls of the Fortifications think. But way out here, past the borders? Beyond the Wasteland where the water tastes like piss and the sun sets red? You'd best believe that all them monsters dear Mommy warned you about ain't just bogeymen she made up to keep you in line."

Orcs were no more real than gold-shitting unicorns. Obviously, this creep was just having his fun. I didn't deign to respond. Of course I didn't.

But I must have let some small, disdainful noise escape me.

The guard pressed himself against my cage, dagger out, daring me to make a lunge for him. "You think one of them beast's gonna care about your snooty ways?" he growled. "The only use they got for horses is as pack animals—and you hardly need some fancy trainer to teach their mules to dance. Unless one takes you for a bedboy." His eyes went nasty. "Pound the attitude outta you with a prick the size of my arm."

The threat of being bought by orcs was ludicrous. Though, frankly, I had no idea why he'd even bothered embellishing the tale. Being sold off to a group of bloodthirsty marauders like the one who'd brought us there would be bad enough— though hopefully they'd find a highly trained horseman less disposable than some poor wench.

I slid a silent apology to the woman in the cage beside me even as I thought it…and did my best not to let my worries show on my face. Animals can read fear in even the smallest of our gestures. But humans will always fall for a confident front.

Unfortunately, not all of them appreciate it. Especially not the ones who get off on others cowering before them. Bollocks rattled my cage hard enough that even I flinched, and said, "Maybe when they're done with ya, I'll scoop you up myself."

I thought the guard was turning to walk away, smug in the notion that he'd planted his hateful little threat, and so it took me entirely by surprise when, instead, he reared back and hawked.

The gob of spit landed beneath my eye, hot and vile. For a heartbeat, I couldn't move—couldn't breathe. If he'd dared such a thing within the walls of the Fortifications, I would've whipped him myself.

But my whip was long gone. I was in a cage. And the Fortifications were leagues away.

As Bollocks strode off, chuckling to himself, something nudged me in the arm. "Here." The woman in the next cage—the one who believed in orcs—was pressing a scrap of cloth between the bars. "I'm Bess."

"Quinn." The sound of my own name felt clumsy in my mouth. I hadn't spoken it since the slavers scooped me up at the edge of the Wasteland a fortnight ago. "My name is Quinn."

Bess nudged me again with her handkerchief, but I waved it away, unwilling to take her only earthly possession. I wiped away the spit with the back of my sleeve instead.

Bess was barely out of her teens, though a hard life had worn a leery crease between her eyebrows. Her brown hair was clipped short, as if she'd recently sold it off to a wigmaker. "Is that right, what he said?" she asked—and I expected her to wonder if orcs were real. "You train horses?"

I hardly felt like much of a horseman on this side of the bars. I gave a vague gesture in reply.

"You can't act like you're still in the Fortifications," she said. "Out here in the Wasteland—sometimes it's best not to brag."

I quirked an eyebrow. "Did I brag? How'd I manage that without speaking so much as a word?"

"I'm just trying to help you," she whispered as another guard passed within earshot. Once he was gone, she added, "Folks can brag plenty without saying a thing. The way you stand there with your chin up. The way you were holding his stare. People like you—the guards like to knock you down a peg. Like when slavers brought me here, just a few days before you, there was a handmaid from a real fancy house. She always got it way worse than the rest of us...if you know what I mean."

I hitched my eyebrow higher.

"Just trying to help," she repeated.

"Why bother?" a younger guy called out from a few cages down. His voice was raspy and dry. "We're all as good as dead."

3

QUINN

"Y'know what? Forget I said anything." Bess curled up in the far corner of her cage—which wasn't very far at all—leaned back against the bars, and shut her eyes.

Honestly, there was a grain of truth to what she'd been trying to tell me. I never backed down from a challenge. If it ever got out that I laid with men, I'd figured, I couldn't afford to look weak. Not only did I need to be the best at trimming a hoof, at correcting a stubborn gait, at gentling a stallion...I had to be utterly above caring what any of the others thought of me. Maybe it was no way to make friends. But at least I enjoyed a grudging respect.

For all the good it did me.

Before I could admit Bess was right, a new guard stomped in, and then another, and soon the reeking tent was buzzing with activity. The sleazy trader in his ridiculous soiled finery was flinging orders faster than his men could follow.

"Give the labor an extra ration. No one's gonna buy 'em if they're collapsed on the bottom of their cages. Oil up the catamites. Put the pretty girls toward the back, so we can offload the sorry ones to the horny bastards who grab the first piece of ass they see. And make sure they got their tits out." He paused in the middle of the tent and waved an arm in my general direction. "Set that one aside—he'll fetch a good price from the Blood Nomads."

Orcs might be nothing more than a fairy tale, but Blood Nomads were, unfortunately, very real. I'd met one myself in the market square. The trader was right—they *could* use my skills, as they practically lived on horseback. But during the drought season, they survived on coagulated loaves of animal blood—horse, cow, even camel—which, over generations, they'd somehow developed the ability to digest. Outsiders couldn't say the same. And even if I did survive the lean months, their meandering travel patterns would take me farther from the Fortifications than I already was. I couldn't let the nomads carry me off if I ever hoped to get back to civilization.

One of the guards paused to squint at the cages, scratching his armpit. "Which one did he say?"

I pointed at a new "recruit" who was sleeping off a bender. "Him."

Lucky for me the guard wasn't Bollocks, who would have known damn well I was the one the trader had meant. They dragged the hungover guy's cage outside, then hauled poor Bess, with her cropped hair, toward the front with the other, less desirable "merchandise." I averted my eyes to allow her some scrap of dignity. Once her cage was gone, I could see the guy who'd spoken before, the one with the raspy voice. He was even younger than I'd imagined—better looking, too, with striking coppery hair. But a bruise in the shape of a handprint covered his left cheek. And when he saw me staring, he replied with a weary smirk.

"You should go with the Nomads," he said. "Otherwise, you'll be shipped off to the copper mines on the coast."

Even farther from the Fortifications. And even harder to escape.

A toothless old man approached the redhead's cage with a bucket and rag. "All right, Archie." He was businesslike, even bored, as he wet the same rag that had been used on every other slave he'd seen so far. "Clean up."

Archie swabbed himself down and said, "Should I get my tits out, too?"

The old man had a few crude cosmetics with him, and while a dusting of rouge wouldn't do much to hide the print on Archie's face, it did make his skin seem less peaked. "You're a mouthy one, aintcha?" He gestured toward the ruddy, five-fingered mark. "Now you'll end up with someone who likes to rough 'em up."

Archie shrugged. "Then at least it'll be over fast."

The old man hauled his bucket over to me, squinting. "Well. Look at you. You're getting a bit long in the tooth for a bedboy."

I was thirty—not a hundred and thirty—though that was nearly twice the age of the shivering catamites doing their best to look brave.

If I wanted to take my chances with the Blood Nomads, the time to speak up was now. Or, for that matter, to demand my extra rations and be dumped in with the laborers.

But anyone wealthy enough to own a pleasure slave would have ties to the Fortifications. Just two weeks ago, I'd been desperate to escape those walls. Now they seemed like paradise...and playing a whore was the only chance I stood at getting back home. So, I imitated Archie's careless shrug, and sealed my fate. "Men might claim they're looking for virgins—but what they really want is someone who knows how to handle a dick."

I could only speak for myself, of course...but it must have rung true enough. The old man shoved the rag at me. I was filthy, both from my time on the road and my time in captivity. Maybe the wipe-down helped. Maybe not. At least I could chafe the spit from my cheek.

"Not many good years left," the old man said as I reflexively blinked against the kohl he smeared under my eyes. He followed it up with a dusting of ground mica across my cheekbones and a daub of rouge on each nipple. "But that clever mouth might keep you fed once your bloom fades."

I looked ridiculous. But I preferred the makeup to an iron collar and a pickaxe.

Once the man had moved on, Archie said, "You're lucky you're pretty enough—and it doesn't hurt that he's half blind. Stand in the shadows and maybe someone will cough up a few pieces of silver for you."

Even less than I'd got for poor Mercy.

I wasn't sure I'd even sell for that, as it was doubtful I could escape closer scrutiny. If the slave trade was anything like the horse auctions I was familiar with, they'd not only be leaning in to check my teeth, but heft my balls.

Activity in the tent was already chaotic. The trader's shouted orders got more urgent as the disorganized guards shuffled and re-shuffled our cages. Some of the catamites and whores were crying now. Some of the laborers too. Soon the sound of tack and harness grew louder, with the crack of a whip and a creak of wagon wheels as the caravan pulled in.

"Can you see?" one of the younger boys called over to Archie, who'd mashed himself against the far side of his cage to peer through a gap in the tent walls. "What's out there?"

Archie craned his neck. "What do you think? Wagons."

"But the drivers," the boy said dramatically. "Are they, y'know...*people*?"

"Hush." Archie waved him off like a persistent fly. "All I see is the stupid back of a guard's stupid head."

We didn't have long to wonder about the potential buyers as a guard flung the tent flaps wide. After days in the dim light under the tarps, my eyes teared as the sun's glare flooded my vision with a dazzling white haze. Once I could finally get a proper look, I picked out men filing in, all of them dusty from their long trek across the Wasteland. But beneath the grit of travel, their clothes were sturdy and well-made. Anyone with enough coin for a slave—let alone passage on a caravan—would hardly be dressed in rags.

Not one of them was without a conspicuous weapon. Several carried more than one.

Of course they did. Life outside the Fortifications was not for the faint of heart. I sized up a spear, imagining how it would feel piercing me between the shoulder blades as I attempted to run from my new "masters." I had to remind myself I wasn't planning to escape yet, anyhow. Not until I was back in civilization.

The buyers filed past, barely skimming me with their bland, assessing looks. My ego has always been healthy, and even so, by the time a half dozen had passed by without so much as a pause, I reminded myself I was no bedboy. I just needed a ticket out of this damned tent.

One of the buyers was obviously quite well-to-do, judging by the quality of his boots and the fat gold chain around his neck. A few of the pleasure slaves attempted to flirt—not Archie, I noted. And not Bess, either. The buyer glanced at me for a fraction of a heartbeat—then bought a pair of terrified youths.

Maybe I really was too old for this, after all.

And evidently, all the pickup moves that worked so well in a tavern—a sly look, a secret smile—were of no use at all in a slaver's tent. One by one, the slave cages thinned out. Picky buyers knew to look toward the back. Tight-fisted buyers shopped toward the front. There were as many types of buyers as there were slaves...though none of them were *my* buyers.

As the day wore on and bartering grew more desperate, I couldn't help but worry that maybe my buyer had somehow missed the caravan. Or, worse, that he was the shady man lurking around the fringes waiting for the prices to go down as trading came to a close.

Soon, there was only a handful of prisoners left, and the haggling started to get ugly. I might very well end up in the distant copper mines after all. Or chained spread-eagle to the axle of the trader's wagon, where Bollocks could start putting his spit to a more creative use...and that's only if he bothered to wet himself with anything at all before he jammed himself up my ass.

I arched my back to thrust out my rump, made sure my shirt had fallen open just so, and did my best to look fuckable and non-threatening...and was still passed up for a whimpering boy covered in snot. *I'll have you know that in the Fortifications, I was considered quite the catch.* By the men who didn't hate themselves for bedding another man, anyhow.

"It's the copper mines for us all," Archie sighed. "Maybe I can pitch myself down an old shaft before I get passed around to all the foremen."

Bess was still there, too. But she was somehow finding the strength to rally. "Hold on—do you hear that? It's another wagon!"

Without the telltale jingle of the harness and crack of the whip, I'd taken the stony rumble for the threat of distant thunder. Now that I really listened, though, I could just make out the creak of heavy wheels.

Negotiations fell silent as something huge pulled up to the tent, blotting out the lowering sun, and casting the silhouettes of the milling people outside into darkness. The cheapskates who'd been hoping to grab someone to work or fuck to death for a pittance scrambled to close on their last offer, but the trader in his ragged silks was no longer listening. Not with a fresh customer bringing up the rear.

The distinctive snort of oxen reached my ears, and the rumble of deep voices. No wonder this latecomer hadn't been with the caravan. The beasts wouldn't be able to keep pace with the lighter horses—but they could plod along for hours on end dragging massive amounts of weight.

What could they be—farmers? Not out here where the soil was so fallow. Stonecutters? A skilled trade, though I supposed they'd need workers to haul the stone.

As I racked my brain imagining who'd just shown up, silhouettes of the outside crowd shifted on the wall of the tent, playing out like shadow theater. But something was wrong. At first, I thought the biggest forms were just far away, their size a trick of perspective. But they were too sharp, too distinct—as clear as the people standing right outside. My gut twisted. They weren't distant at all. They were close. And they were huge.

The tent flap was shut to keep out both the flies and the punishing heat of the day. I was baffled when one of the new figures (which should have still been several paces away, judging by the sheer size) flung it open wide.

Daylight knifed through the opening. Acclimated to the darkness, my eyes were dazzled. I blinked away spots—and flecks of kohl, no doubt—and blinked again, unable to make sense of what I was seeing.

Though there was no mistaking the moment Archie's bravado slipped, and a guttural sound worked its way up from his throat. And the soft thud of Bess dropping to the floor of her cage as she fainted dead away.

My vision finally cleared as a giant of a man stooped down to duck through the tent's opening and come inside.

No...not a man, I realized, taking in the greenish cast to his skin, bulge of tusks jutting from his mouth, and the sheer size of him.

An orc.

"Hey, hey you!" Archie waved vigorously, trying to get the attention of the unsavory man lurking on the sidelines. "Get me out of here and I promise you won't regret it! However you want it, whatever messed-up shit you're into—I'm your guy."

But the man wasn't about to get into a bidding war. Not with an *orc*. He slipped out from the tent to rejoin the caravan.

As we've established, I wasn't born yesterday—and so, obviously, I knew better than to stare. No creature I've ever studied reacted well to direct eye contact...but I just couldn't help myself. The thing was massive—easily four hands taller than me and wider than any two men. A horse would buckle under such weight. No wonder they used oxen.

Its brow was low and its jaws were strong, powerful enough to handle tough plants...or, judging by the tusks, crush bones. Its hide was green and dappled like forest shade, thick but smooth as polished leather. And though it was huge—bigger than any beast I'd ever seen walk on two legs—it moved with deadly purpose.

And it wore wealth like a king.

"Get a load of those rubies around his neck," Archie whispered. "He can take the whole lot of us back to wherever he came from—and the tent too."

The creature paused, great nostrils dilating, broad chest heaving as it scented the air.

Horses are pack animals. Prey animals. As a horseman, it was always important to establish myself as the leader of their herd...but I had never felt like prey myself.

Until now.

I stilled so the creature's small eyes would miss me in the gloom of the tent, though if it did have my scent, all the stillness in the world wouldn't help me. Hopefully, that scent would somehow be lost amidst the mingled stink of so many poorly washed bodies.

Another great beast of an orc ducked through the high tent flap and joined the first, this one a slightly paler green, with a long scar at the corner of his mouth—an old wound healed into a craggy ridge that pulled his tusked face into a permanent grin. His tusks were even bigger, tipped with decorative silver caps.

The two orcs conferred briefly. And when their heads swiveled in the direction of the pleasure slaves where only Archie, Bess and I remained, I realized my hopes of blending in were fruitless.

4

MAROK

Borkul scanned the human slaves—the straggling remainders who'd been passed up by their own kind. "You've been alone too long, Marok," he told me. "What's stopping you from getting a slave of your own?"

Of all my clan, he should understand the most. It was his sister who I lost to the wandering troll.

"We're not here for me." I said, curt.

"No. But you can afford it—and our chieftain would say the same. A warrior who gets too much in his head is no good for the clan. Especially a general, like you. And you're so far in your own head, it's a wonder you can't see backwards." He thumbed the ridge over his tusk and took the scent of the offerings. The smell of humans will tell you a lot, if you take the time to read it. Age. Sex. Feeding habits. Fertility. And, of course, fear—though a good warrior will scent fear on every foe.

"You don't know how the chieftain would react," I said. "He has no reason to show me any tolerance. Not after what happened." The troll had taken Akala from both Borkul and me. That wound we shared.

The chieftain's contempt over my failures was mine alone to bear.

Why would the chieftain forgive me? He wasn't my heart-brother. Though neither was Borkul, now that the ashes from Akala's pyre were lost to the wind. But Borkul still treated me like a brother, all the same.

When he approached the pleasure slaves, I kept to his side. Of those humans that remained, at least half carried the stagnant taint of disease. Most had one rotten tooth, many had more. And one of them was bleeding somewhere inside its soft belly. In my opinion, these fragile beings made the worst concubines. But that was why they were in demand. To keep such a weak and frivolous thing alive for the sheer sake of its company was the ultimate sign of prestige.

I'd rather have a kitten. At least it would grow up to fend for itself...and rid my home of the lizards always managing to sneak in.

Borkul paused beside a prone female, and when he took her scent, so did I. Not only was she still alive, but surprisingly healthy.

The tendency to lose consciousness in the face of a threat. Yet another human trait that had me baffled.

"This one seems like it's in good shape." Borkul prodded her in the thigh.

"No handling the wares," said a male in strangely colored silks, rushing over. Tough words. But he reeked of fear. "You break it, you buy it."

Borkul ignored him and poked the female again. She stirred, and her fear perfumed the air. "Speak," he said as her eyelids fluttered open.

She scrambled toward the back of her cage and squeaked, "Me?"

"Again," he demanded.

"I—ah—" she began to cry. Her tears smelled of the sea.

"She might be addled," Borkul murmured. "It would explain why she was face-down on the floor."

"Please," she sobbed. "Please don't pick me."

I shrugged. She seemed of sound mind to me—but the chieftain wasn't looking for a concubine to distract him. He had enough problems with the Two Swords Clan sniffing around our eastern border. He just needed a few able-bodied slaves to perform certain tasks we couldn't. I wasn't so sure we'd have any luck finding them. The pickings looked slim this late in the day, but the shaman had insisted we come.

Borkul scanned a few stripling males—not yet grown, so they might adapt better to the clan if they survived. Even for humans, though, they seemed frail and weak. We could hardly afford the years it would take to nurture them into something useful.

I was about to drag Borkul over to the laborers, but found that he'd stopped to consider one of the males. His scent was oddly sour, like he was fighting off a malady, possibly to the throat. But overall, he was healthy enough. Ordinary. Unremarkable.

Except for the sign of the augur on his cheek—the Red Hand.

"Come over here," Borkul demanded. "Let me see you."

"Why not?" The boy heaved herself off the back of the cage with a sigh—yes, the ague was in his lungs—and presented himself at the bars. "You'll take me whether or not I play along."

Borkul looked him up and down, then settled on the augur sign. "How did you come by that mark on your face?"

"The same way you 'came by' your scar, I'd wager—though with a much blunter object. Guess I should be glad for small favors."

I puzzled over his words for a moment until I recalled something I'd once heard about his kind. "It's no sign," I told Borkul. "It's just temporary. These creatures are so soft, they bruise like fruit."

He grunted his disappointment...but even though he knew I was right, he still couldn't keep his eyes off the shape of the hand. "Even if it does fade, you must admit, his hair is the right color. It seems lucky."

The small male barked a cynical laugh, then succumbed to a fit of coughing.

"He is weak," I said.

Borkul disagreed. "Maybe now, but he might recover. And he has fight."

"You make the choice," I said. My own judgment was clearly worthless.

As Borkul turned toward the trader to begin his negotiations, he went still, homing in on another scent. Despite my unwillingness to involve myself in this decision, I followed suit. There, standing very calm and exceedingly still, just behind the slave with the false augur's mark, was an older male. There was no illness on his scent, no rot, and very little fear. His exposed chest was well-muscled—for a human—and his temperament was intriguingly dignified.

I nudged Borkul and said, "That one would at least make it back to the clan."

The faint fear smell grew stronger.

At least the male wasn't stupid.

Borkul thumbed his scar—his thinking-habit—and eventually said, "And the chieftain can use him however he deems fit."

"You don't want me," the male said with surprising authority.

"Shut your mouth," the trader snapped.

Borkul, ignoring the trader, snorted in amusement. "I don't? And why is that?"

"Because I'm obviously a poor excuse for a bedboy—I'm far too old."

The dark-haired male hardly looked past his prime to me—but what did I know? If their soft flesh never meets with the end of a weapon, humans can live a surprisingly long time—especially if they're not exposed to sickness. Curious now, I eased in to better take his scent. Underneath the typical musk and sweat, it was clean. His teeth were whole. His lungs were clear. And...interesting. Farther down, beneath the kiss of old campfire smoke and traces of the last meal he ate, was the unmistakable whiff of horse.

Nothing to read into. He'd likely been delivered to the slaver thrown over the rump of a pack animal.

Borkul began negotiations for the slave with the augur mark while I stood by, silent, tasting the air.

Was that the rich smoothness of saddle leather I scented?

No doubt it meant nothing. I turned away to head over to the laborers and see if there were any worth buying, but the slaver intercepted, babbling that surely we'd want to present our chieftain with the widest variety of pleasures. I sidestepped to avoid flattening him, which pressed me face-up to the bars of the male's cage. The male's fear scent spiked, and a knot in his throat bobbed as he swallowed. "You don't want me," he repeated, with only a hint of a tremor in his voice. "I'd be a total waste of your good coin."

"Oh?" I said.

"That's right. Absolutely nothing to offer that any orc worth his mettle would want."

I was intrigued by the way he carried himself, straight and proud, and the way his sleek muscles bunched and corded so impressively...for a soft human. There was a spark of intelligence in his eyes that matched his sure stance. Such a slave would either be a very wise choice—or a very risky one. A slave who could think for himself could be quite an asset compared to a dullard who simply followed orders. Though if he turned on you, he'd be far more dangerous.

The slaver and Borkul stepped away to barter in earnest for the others, leaving me staring at the dark-haired male.

"I'd be utterly useless in bed," he assured me. "In fact, I'm not even a pleasure slave at all."

Everyone knows humans are liars. I supposed that made me curious what would come out of his mouth next. "Ah. If you're no pleasure slave, then what are you?"

He tilted his chin up and squared his shoulders. "I'm a horseman."

Humans might lie with words—but never with scent. And my nose told me that his claim was true.

I'd lost hope of ever taking back my rightful place in the clan...of being treated once again as a warrior instead of a disgrace. But if I was the one who could end a decade of war, the chieftain would shun me no longer. And this human could very well be the key to winning that conflict for good.

As I stepped back, his fear scent gave way to a flood of relief. He thought I was leaving, not realizing I was just grabbing the slaver's attention. Though he kenned well enough to the situation when I raised my voice, pointed directly at his painted chest, and called out, "I'll take him."

5

QUINN

After days of being caged, spat on, painted, and displayed like merchandise, I thought I'd seen the worst.

Then I had an iron collar clamped around my neck and got paraded to an orcish wagon in chains.

The other leftovers were with me. I was in the middle, with Archie plodding along resolutely in front and Bess bringing up the rear as she quietly choked back tears. I wished I could offer her a word of encouragement, but I had none. At least I'd left her with her handkerchief.

The oxen were the biggest I'd ever seen, and the wagon where they were yoked must weigh a literal ton, from the tight-grained lumber of the bed to the massive iron wheels. The more gregarious orc was still chatting with the slaver, while the dour, pensive orc—the one who'd picked me— hauled us outside. He didn't seem to be dragging us along on purpose, but his stride was huge. By the time we reached the wagon, Archie was taken by a coughing fit and Bess was openly sobbing. The big brute of an orc glared down at us, then hoisted up Archie effortlessly and set him in back with pragmatic finality.

Since we were chained together, I didn't see much choice but to follow—but, damn it, I'd do so on my own terms. I dodged the orc as much as I could without collapsing my own windpipe, then swung up into the wagon of my own volition. At least from there I could offer Bess a hand up and spare her the groping of an orc...if only for the time being.

Chests and crates filled the wagon beneath its hide cover. There was nowhere to sit but the wooden floor, but Archie found a gap between the supplies where we could tuck ourselves away. The chains linking our collars were long enough to let us move around a bit—probably so we could work—but not long enough to forget they were there.

Bess dried her tears, sniffled, and said, "Where d'you suppose they're taking us?"

Archie smiled with no humor whatsoever. "What difference does it make? You saw the size of them. By morning we'll be split wide open from being pounded with their fat orcish dongs."

"Speak for yourself," I snapped.

Archie's eyes crinkled. "Well, maybe not you, horseman. Maybe you already know your way around a freakish big dong...."

"Shut up, both of you," Bess sobbed. "We can't afford to fight. Once they take us back to wherever it is they live, then all we'll have is each other."

True enough.

Soon, the wagon creaked as an orc hauled himself into the driver's seat and we all fell silent. The wheels shuddered the wagon bed as we rolled out of the slaver camp and left its stinking tents behind.

Exactly how long we traveled, I couldn't quite say. I was accustomed to putting in long hours, both at work, and carousing afterward. My captivity seemed both painfully long and strangely bleary, with days of enforced inactivity blending together. This journey, at least, was something new. We traveled for a long while at a slow and steady plod, pausing only to water the oxen. The crumbling, pale soil of the Wasteland eventually gave way to tentative scrubland, and eventually, trees. Some, I recognized. But peppered among them were strange, spiny things the likes of which I'd never imagined.

The orcs spoke to each other with voices like stone, too low to make out much. Debating whether to stop, from what I could glean. Archie didn't share any more premonitions about meeting his fate impaled on an orcish dick. But when he met my eyes, I knew that's what he must be thinking.

Full darkness fell, and the chirp of insects joined the creaking wheels and occasional scraps of our captors' conversation as our view out the back of the wagon faded. I'd been lulled into a fitful half-sleep when I jolted into awareness at the distant sound of a fiddle.

Playing a drinking song I knew all too well.

The wagon rolled to a stop. The darkness outside was painted orange by flickering torchlight, and in the distance, I heard the murmur of a crowd. A settlement, then. Not the Fortifications—an orc would never get past the gate—but some frontier town where our captors might pass unremarked.

If there was ever a perfect opportunity to run away, it was now. Even with the collars, we could slip away and find a blacksmith to strike the chains from our necks. I leaned in close, having no idea how good the orcs' hearing might be, and said, "We're getting out of here."

Archie scoffed.

I ignored him. "I'll take the lead. When I say run, fall in line behind me and don't look back. We'll lose ourselves among the other people and make our way back home."

"Whose home?" Archie asked.

Did it matter, so long as we were with our own kind again—and none of us ended up as a monster's plaything?

"I'll make for the thickest part of the crowd," I said. "And who knows? If we're lucky, someone might help us."

"There's that word again," Archie said...and he didn't need to point out that if any of us were even remotely lucky, we wouldn't have ended up here in the first place.

The wagon groaned as the orcs hopped down, and their shadows loomed large against the tarp. The one with the scar and the silver-tipped tusks appeared at the foot of the wagon bed, gesturing. "Out, and grab those bedrolls on the way. Relieve yourselves downwind and set up camp."

The bedding was heavy, canvas stuffed with straw. I took one, while Archie and Bess struggled the other down between them. It was awkward work, made worse by the chains...which gave me an idea. "It would go a lot faster without the collars," I suggested.

To which the orc barked a single laugh.

The other orc, the quiet, serious one, grabbed hold of the chain and walked us over to a stand of trees. He crossed his arms, bored, as he waited for us to empty our bladders. If Bess was ever embarrassed about squatting in front of two men and an orc, she was numb to it now after so many days of availing herself of an old bucket, just like all the rest of the unfortunate captives.

"Cover it," the orc said sharply as we turned to walk back to camp. We all paused, confused. "Cover your stink," he said, like he was speaking to a bunch of simpletons.

Even if it weren't dark, I can't imagine we would have any chance of finding the exact spot where we'd pissed. But we made our best attempt and dutifully kicked around a bunch of dead leaves.

When we got back to the clearing, the scarred orc was rummaging through a chest of supplies. He handed a wineskin to the quiet one and said, "What's it to be? Shopping or guard duty?"

"We have what we came for," the quiet one said.

"Maybe so, Marok, but I smell venison—can you really pass that up?"

Marok? Was that a name? It sounded like one. Why was I so surprised the orcs had names? Hell, even the trained pigeons my old neighbor used to keep had names. I listened, and learned Marok was the stern, quiet orc and Borkul had the horrific scar.

They'd parked in a clearing that had obviously been used by many travelers before us, though not particularly well. A firepit with a spit was dug in the center, and the area all around it was littered with refuse. No Fortifications wall in sight, so we must have been at one of the more distant way station camps. And in the distance, people milled about a ragtag setup of tables and tents at a makeshift night market.

"Set up the camp," Borkul told us. "Unless you like sleeping on a pile of trash in the cold."

"Maybe they don't know how to make a fire," Marok said doubtfully.

"Of course I do," Archie snapped. "I'm not an idiot."

Working together, the three of us made a stack of twigs, lit it with orcish tinder, then fed the small flames with the shattered remains of a broken crate. There was plenty of fuel littering the campsite. But not all of the scraps were wood.

"Bones," Archie said with a shudder as he tossed what looked like a calf's femur toward the edge of the clearing. "So many bones."

"What kind of bones?" Bess said, voice hushed.

"The bones of idle slaves," Borkul called over. Damn. Their hearing was a lot better than I'd thought.

I located a rib, far too big to be any natural person's. Although, maybe it was from an orc.... I glanced at our captors. No. The ribcage was shaped all wrong. More likely a boar. "They're not human," I told Bess. "The bones, I mean."

She looked dubious.

"Think," I said. "It's a campfire. So this is just what's left of someone's dinner. Animals. Nothing worse."

"Unless there were trolls here before us," Borkul called over, then snorted derisively. "If so, who knows what the poor sods might've once been?"

We stopped talking after that. While I built up the fire, Archie chucked bones into the darkness, and Bess gathered twigs as she knuckled away silent tears.

I supposed wanting both orcs to go to the market and leave us a way out was too much to hope for. But if they at least separated, between the three of us, maybe we could overpower a single orc. Archie was just about to figure out how far he could pitch another rib, but seeing the shape of it, I stopped him. It was slimmer than the first we'd found, just shorter than his forearm, and it tapered dangerously toward the tip. Even unsharpened, it might do some damage. I felt around until my hand closed over another stray rib protruding from the sandy soil.

So many bones.

But that meant I was able to find another weapon.

My heart hammered in my chest as I realized what we were about to do. Wringing the neck of a stewing hen was one thing, but I'd never stabbed anyone. The orc that called himself Marok might not be a person, exactly, but he spoke words and thought thoughts. He had a name.

Desperate times. A life in chains would be bad enough. A life being plowed open by these great beasts, however short, was even worse.

I wouldn't risk words, not with the orcs' sharp hearing. But no matter how good their senses might be, they couldn't see through my body. I put my back to them and gripped the pointy rib like a dagger to show the others what I meant to do. They both nodded their understanding.

By the time the scarred orc had gone off in the direction of the night market, I'd found a third good weapon, a sturdy leg bone broken to a vicious, sharp point. While I fussed over the fire, Archie watched Marok, the quiet one, indicating which way the orc had gone with a flick of the eyes. When Archie gave us the nod, we surged to our feet, aiming for the far side of the market, and broke into a run.

Most creatures who have size to their advantage are not particularly quick. Like the oxen now tethered beside the campsite, what they gained in size and strength, they lost in speed.

But apparently, not orcs.

One moment, Marok was squatting on the ground with his back to a wagon wheel, cleaning off a bit of tack. The next, he was on his feet and heading straight for us.

It was clear that no matter how fast we ran, we'd soon be overtaken. And so, instead of running away, I tightened my grip on the sharpened bone, adjusted my angle, and ran toward the orc.

The chains on my iron collar snapped taut as my fellow captives fought my change of course. But if we didn't work together, we'd be dead—and after a brief resistance, they followed my lead. Together, the three of us charged the oncoming orc.

6

QUINN

With all my courage—with all my desperation and strength, and my last hope of ever finding my way home—I drew back the bone blade, and I swung. The blow landed hard on the side of the orc's tree-trunk neck. For a brief moment, I wondered if his blood would run red like a man's. But there was no hesitation in the swing.

Yet though the point struck true, the bone blade didn't pierce his hide.

It simply shattered.

"Run," I called out, as the orc cocked his head, puzzled, then brushed the bone shards from his leathers.

Why he wasn't chasing, I didn't stop to wonder. Having hit him—however ineffectively—I'd sealed my fate. Now, it was either run...or die.

Fueled by fear, Archie and Bess ran hard, just as hard as

me, blundering in the dark over scrubby ground. But the lights of the settlement beckoned, and soon we could see the tents, and read the signs, and even count the people. There were scores of people there—maybe even a few hundred—and surely once we were among our own kind, we'd be safe.

Our feet found a path and we ran harder still.

The path led us toward a night market lined by tables on either side, with barkers all shouting over each other, trying to entice their potential customers. Meat sizzled on a spit nearby. A man's drunken singing carried over the crowd. It was loud and raucous, but it was more like home than anything I'd seen since I'd joined the wool merchants' caravan.

Surely among all these people we'd find help—someone to strike off these blasted collars, a merchant willing to hide us in their tent. Our captors were orcs and we were human, and that had to count for something.

The first stall along the thoroughfare was piled with metal, from cookware to weapons, and though the vendor had his back to us, I could tell by the broadness of his shoulders that he'd be just the one to free us from our irons. "Sir," I called out to him. "Good Sir, we need your—"

My voice dried up to a croak as he turned and fixed us with a beady stare—from only one eye. Half his face was covered in hanging skin, obscuring one side of his features, while the other half, the staring half, was smooth and taut. His nose leaned off-kilter, and the single visible eye had a pupil square as a goat's.

I'd once seen a man utterly disfigured by fire—but that wouldn't explain his eye. My collar tugged as Bess backpedaled, while Archie murmured, "Holy hell."

The man slammed a hand on his table so hard that the

stacks of cooking pots all jumped. Not a human hand, but a reptilian claw.

"What're you looking at?" he demanded—amused, even mocking. But the three of us were already staggering away.

The crowd flowed and parted around us, no one seeming to notice or care that we were in chains. It didn't matter. Because up close, I saw, none of them were fully human.

There were tall creatures and short, fat and thin, furred and scaled and everything in between. They stood like men, dressed like men, and even caroused and bartered like men.

But they were most definitely *not* men.

A creature no taller than my shoulder with a dog-like face whuffed out a laugh and pointed in our direction. His studded armor was so heavy, I'd have trouble even standing up in it, let alone dancing the mocking little jig he was doing at our expense. A tall, sallow thing with eyes sunk deep in his skull treated us to a rude gesture. Everywhere I looked— monsters. Then I spotted a human shape in the crowd. Just a normal man, not horned or scaled or furred. I dragged the others toward him, calling out, "Sir, please, help us—"

He turned to see who was bothering him, and took us in with calm, glinting eyes...set close and canny, over the snout of a pig.

The crowd sensed us now—sensed that we were not like them—and even more of the creatures began to not only take notice, but to point and jeer. Archie and Bess crowded in on either side of me, as if I had any way to protect them. A stumpy, gray-skinned thing looped a string of sausages around his neck and mockingly cried, "Help me, good sir! Help me!" while the others roared with laughter.

"So that's what all the ruckus is about," remarked a

familiar, deep voice as the orc called Borkul shouldered his way through the crowd. He caught the end of the chain that bound us together and shook his head ruefully. "You won't find much help here," he said, completely unperturbed. "Humans have enslaved the kin of most everyone here. Your people would sell off their own brother if they thought they'd turn a profit. Come on, then. Might as well make yourselves useful while you're here."

He loaded me down with a heavy crate, while piling random smaller purchases on Archie and Bess. By the time we staggered back to the campsite, my shoulders were burning and my back complained. Once we set down the supplies by the wagon, I said, "It was my idea to run. I didn't give the others any choice about it. So if you're going to whip anyone—"

"Saucy little things," Bokul said jovially to his fellow orc, "aren't they?"

Marok answered with a rumbly sigh.

"Too bad we can't take a wee taste," Borkul added as Bess tensed beside me and my blood ran cold.

Marok gave his head a curt shake. "I'm in bad enough standing as it is without rubbing my scent all over the chieftain's slaves."

"True," Borkul agreed. "It's just been too long since I've scratched that itch."

"I'm sure someone in the market will oblige," Marok said.

"I'm sure they will," Borkul said slyly. "And I'm sure, for the right price, they'd be happy to bring a friend."

Marok gave a disdainful snort and hefted one of the heavy bedrolls one-handed. He snapped it open with a single jerk, and it unrolled as easily as a silken party streamer.

"Come on," Borkul chided, "I saw some fetching goblins

loitering around the red lantern."

"Have at it, then. I'll take first watch."

Borkul watched Marok shake open the second bedroll, smile fading as he went serious. "Akala wouldn't have wanted you to go the rest of your life without—"

"I'm in no mood for goblins," Marok snapped. "That's all."

Borkul shrugged. "More for me."

Once the scarred orc had ambled off toward the night market, Marok pointed to a massive fallen log. It hadn't been there before, so he must have dragged it over. And judging by the way the oxen were currently dozing in a nearby patch of grass, he'd done so himself, without their help.

"Sit," he commanded, and the three of us shuffled over and dutifully sat. Hefting an iron mallet, he drove a tapered tent spike into the last chain link, fastening us all to the log. "Just in case you still think there's anywhere to run."

We waited in silence as he went through the purchases Borkul made, then thrust a loaf of bread into the hands of the nearest captive—who happened to be Archie. We'd been given nothing but a thin, greasy gruel that day, and at the sight of the bread, my stomach twisted in eager anticipation. "There was meat for you too," Marok said. "But since we can't trust you with a knife, you'll have to make do with the bread."

Archie ripped off a corner and stuffed it in his mouth before he broke the loaf into rough thirds. As fatalistic as he might come off, that boy was a survivor through and through.

I'd eaten at fine tables before, but the stale, coarse bread clutched in my fist was the best damn thing I'd ever tasted. I knew I should take it slow, but instead, I devoured it, every last bite. Marok, on the other side of the fire, crouched on his haunches. The position hardly looked comfortable to me—but was obviously practical, as it would let him spring to his feet at the first sign of trouble.

"Wouldn't trust the meat anyway," Archie whispered as he gathered the last few crumbs from his shirt with a wet fingertip. "Who knows what it might've once been?"

I wasn't so sure I cared. My portion of bread might have been more generous than anything we'd had at the hands of the slaver, but I was so famished I could have eaten the whole loaf myself.

Our captor had been gazing out into the night as we ate, but soon after we finished eating, he rose in one smooth motion and rounded the fire. Archie froze, and Bess made a small sound of panic as she shrank against me. The orc ignored all of this and simply said, "Stand."

We obeyed, chains clinking.

He grabbed the huge fallen tree by a gnarled root and began dragging it toward the bedrolls—and I realized my fear of him wasn't entirely warranted. Marok hadn't refused a red lantern wench just because he didn't have a taste for goblins.

He wanted the new slaves all to himself.

Thanks to my futile attempt to stab him in the neck, if anyone was getting plowed in half tonight...it would be me. He wore utilitarian armor, metal plated leather, but where a human would have worn a tunic beneath to stop the straps from chafing, his own tough hide sufficed. Through the gaps in the armor, I could see his muscles flex, and I realized just how ridiculous our plan to overpower him actually was. Maybe if we were all strong fighters with armor and weapons. But weak as we were, we didn't stand a chance.

And now we would pay the price.

We stood in a small huddle beside the log—even brazen Archie was trembling now—and awaited our fate with dread. Marok straightened and dusted off his hands. He stared for a moment, then said, "Well, what are you waiting for? Sleep."

Bess cleared her throat, then meekly said, "On the... bedrolls?"

"There's only two," Marok said brusquely. "We'd only set out to buy two humans. You'll have to make do."

It was awkward work with the three of us chained to the fallen tree, but we managed to shove the bedrolls together. Sleeping sideways, we'd certainly fit. But I wondered where the orcs would sleep. No doubt the others were just as confused. And with Marok crouching there within earshot just across the fire, we could hardly discuss the matter.

"Do we set watch?" Bess asked.

"You go right ahead," Archie said. "This is the first time in weeks I've been able to stretch out. I'm going to sleep."

"Get some rest," I told her. While I, too, had spent the last several nights curled up on the floor of a cage, I'd best not get too comfortable. If the orcs decided to teach me a lesson, I fully intended to go down fighting.

7

MAROK

The humans were practically asleep before they hit the bedrolls. How they could sleep on those musty, straw-filled bags of dust was beyond me. No wonder they had no sense of smell if that's how they insisted on spending their nights. I'd cleared spots for Borkul and me where I could keep watch on them. They might not be strong, but if the large one had aimed for my eye instead of my neck, things would've gone much worse.

And I doubted he'd make the same mistake twice.

The smart thing would be to sell him off at the bazaar before he caught me by surprise and drove a stick into my brain. I would have already sold him by now, if not for his expertise. Finding a horseman in the slave tents had been an incredible stroke of luck—but like every unexpected boon, it came with a price. Hopefully the cost of this one wouldn't be my eye.

It wasn't long before Borkul ambled back with a goblin under each arm—a male and a female. Goblins don't fall prey to the maladies that plague the weaker races, so their scents were strong and clean, though I could've done without the sandflower essence they'd both liberally applied to their armpits and groins.

"Take your pick," Borkul said—completely ignoring what I'd said about not wanting a goblin.

I had nothing against them—I just wasn't in the mood. I waved him off. "Go have fun. I'll keep watch."

The female goblin batted her long lashes at me. "Come on, big boy, I just filed down my teeth this morning. Y'gonna let all that effort go to waste?"

I threw another log on the fire without reply, and settled in to watch it burn.

Goblins are predators, nearly as big as humans, and their teeth are notoriously brutal. Claws, too—though they say it doesn't hurt nearly as much to blunt them as it does to dull their teeth. Among their own kind, they wouldn't dream of closing their mouth around someone's dick. Not unless they were proving a point on the genitals of a vanquished enemy. Just goes to show what sorts of concessions you have to make when you live in mixed company.

The male goblin was less interested in seduction, likely eager to get on with things so he could head back to the bazaar and turn another trick. His black hair was slicked back in an elaborate knot and multiple hoops glinted from his pointed ears. Probably brass, not gold. But even so, brass wasn't free.

In daylight, the goblins' skin would be the dun clay color of their native soil and not the handsome dappled green of an orc, though in the firelight, they looked more like us than the soft, pale humans did. They were sturdy and sinewy, with the broad foreheads, huge eyes, and pointed chins common to all their kind.

Borkul tried again to get me to join in, but I just shook my head and continued to feed the fire—and eventually he gave up and led the goblins off into the brush. Close enough for me to keep sentry...but far enough for me to ignore the specifics.

Even if we found a stream to bathe in, Borkul would still have sandflower clinging to him by the time he got home. But so long as it wasn't the scent of another orc, his wife had no reason to be annoyed, presuming he brought her a gift that was equal to what he'd spent on the whores.

The goblins were very vocal in their admiration of Borkul's scent, muscles, and cock. It was all an act, but their delivery was enthusiastic enough. And when things really heated up, they seemed to enjoy it. It was possible their eagerness was sincere. Maybe mating with random travelers was easier work than breaking rocks inside whatever mountain they'd come from, ceaselessly digging so their greedy chieftains could expand their clan's territory.

When the transaction was done and the goblins were pulling up their breeches, I shifted my position to keep an eye on the wagon. They might have admired Borkul's cock...but that didn't mean they were above pilfering anything within reach. Goblins are notorious for snagging anything of value on the pointed hooks of their claws. Even clipped blunt, as these two kept theirs, their fingers would still be light.

The female finished dressing first, knotting the ties on her beaded shawl with a lazy nonchalance as she sauntered toward the fire, looking me over. "Well, Mr. Watchkeeper...now that you've had some time to think on it, have you changed your mind about that blowjob?" She was persistent, I'd give her that. And I liked the impish glint in her eye. "Or are you worried you'll pick up the scent of your clanmate's jizz from me, so your wife suspects you're bonking each other?"

Akala.... Any interest that might have been stirring immediately drained away. The space was filled by a pang of loss—followed by the inevitable flood of guilt.

The goblin wench didn't notice my expression. But it was dark. And they're not nearly as cunning as they think they are.

The male came to join her, walking gingerly, and paused beside the fire to scrutinize our three exhausted humans. "How much for the female?"

"She's not for sale," I said.

"Are you sure?" He cocked his head in that peculiar goblin way. With bulging eyes set so wide in their faces, it's a wonder they can't see behind themselves. "Everything's got a price."

Borkul joined us in nothing but his breeches with the scent of sandflower and goblin wafting off his skin. "Of course it does. Uh...what were we talking about?"

"That human there, on the end," the male goblin repeated. "How much?"

Before Borkul could answer, I repeated more firmly, "She is not for sale."

The female goblin fluttered her eyelashes. "Come now, Mr. Watchkeeper...we can offer double what you paid. Surely you could see the advantage of telling your chieftain she slipped off into the night—then pocket the extra coin for yourselves."

"You don't know what we paid," Borkul said, bantering, light.

The male goblin cocked his head the other way. "Ah, but we can guess. We haven't been to the edge of the human settlements ourselves, but we've rutted with enough traders who've passed through. How about this—double the coin, and I'll throw in a sack of fried cave crickets bigger than your head. They're in season, you know. Extra spicy."

Borkul cut his eyes to me. He was tempted—not by the cave crickets, but the coin. It was easy money, and the chieftain was only expecting us to return with two humans anyway. But I couldn't buy my way back into his favor. I had to be the one to end the Two Swords Clan's incursions for good.

I shook my head once, and Borkul shrugged. He ushered the goblins toward the edge of our camp with an easy laugh. "Sorry, my short friends—finders keepers. Though I will be sure to check out those cave crickets before we set off in the morning."

Once the goblins were gone, Borkul joined me to crouch beside the fire. "They seemed pretty keen on the female," he observed. I grunted. "Come to think of it, I didn't notice any human whores by the red lantern."

"So, there's your answer. You know how squeamish humans can be about mating with other races. I'm sure human wenches and bedboys are always in demand."

Borkul scratched an armpit. "And yet, they didn't make an offer for the boy."

"Then they must have plenty of males. Not our problem. If it's human wenches they want, they can go to the slavers themselves. Your watch starts in two hours. Go to sleep."

Since I'd already cleared the ground by the fire and swept it smooth with the branches of a fallen spruce, Borkul didn't need to do anything but lie down and close his eyes. Though he did pause to glance over at our humans and say, "How they manage to sleep on those mushy, lumpy bedrolls, I'll never know."

Soon enough, Borkul rolled onto his belly and started to snore. The distant sounds from the bazaar carried on the night wind. Different races had different ideas of what time was best for sleeping—day or night—so the noise there never really shut down. It just changed in tenor depending on who was awake.

I could find work easily enough in a settlement like that. Merchants were always eager to hire orcish security. What would it be like to live among so many other different races? I suspected that, oddly enough, there'd be a certain anonymity there, even if I was the sole orc in a mass of goblins and mongrels and ogres and whatever else called these streets home. I doubted anyone would stop me from leaving the Red Hand. It was tempting to stay in a place where I didn't need to carry my past on my shoulders.

But fleeing your past is no way to atone for your mistakes.

Lost in thought, I let Borkul sleep an extra hour, then woke him once my eyelids grew heavy. We had too many miles yet to travel, and I needed rest. With one last look at the humans huddled together on their uncomfortable bedrolls, I settled in by the fire to sleep—

—and was pulled from the depths of slumber by the sound of a human shriek.

Our fire hissed as a bucket of water doused it, but not before I spied the silhouette of a half-dozen thieves creeping through our camp—the goblin with the bronze earrings leading the way. Borkul! The thought of him slaughtered in his sleep, just like his sister, brought bile to the back of my throat.

My eyes hadn't quite adjusted to the dark, but I calmed myself with a strong whiff. No scent of blood.

Not yet.

Goblins are tunnelers, and by starlight alone, they can see everything clear as day. They'd doused the fire to give themselves an advantage, since my vision would take a moment to catch up. I groped for the short club I always kept at my side, but it was nowhere. My sword lay with my gear—too long for this tight space—and the club was likely in the hands of the marauding goblins already. My eating knife wouldn't do much good, but I pulled it anyhow. Since I had no desire to be brained by my own weapon, I cast around in the dark for something substantial to defend myself with, but I'd cleared the ground around me for sleeping too well, and there was nothing.

And then Borkul pressed his back to mine in a fighting stance and asked, "How many?"

You'd know damn well if you'd been awake was the obvious answer, but I was too relieved he was still alive to say so. "Five, maybe six."

"They've got my sword," he said, and came up with a splintered plank to defend himself with.

Our humans were awake now. The younger male cried out, "What the—? What *are* they?" Two goblins were already on them, one prying out the tent peg while another tried to wedge open our female's collar.

The tent peg was the first to give, and soon, the end of the chain swung free—but if the goblins thought to drag off our slaves...the humans had other ideas.

The human horseman yanked the chain from the goblin's startled grasp, swinging it in an easy, defensive circle. His stance was firm—he stood like a fighter, not a slave. In the moonlight, his skin didn't look nearly as soft and vulnerable as it had by firelight. I'd been leery of this one when he came at me with a makeshift knife. But I was glad enough for him now, since he was willing to defend the female. Without a decent weapon at hand and so many goblins skulking through our camp, I welcomed the alliance...even if I could only trust him to protect his own kind.

Borkul nudged a signal with his shoulder. We started rounding the firepit in a well-choreographed move, minimizing every vulnerability. A couple of goblins scrambled to cut us off from our humans—Bronze Earring in the lead with an ugly, serrated blade in his hand.

"Come on, now," Borkul said to him. "Is that any way to be? I thought we were pals."

"You should have just sold the wench when you had the chance," the goblin hissed, and swiped at Borkul's knees with the blade. Goblins have a surprisingly long reach, and that blade was just the thing to saw through a tendon. But Borkul sidestepped and gave him a solid whack in the shoulder with his plank.

"Walk away," Borkul said, all playfulness now gone from his voice. "No one needs to die tonight."

Earring wasn't impressed. "You might be big, but you're outnumbered. Give us the female and I'll go easy on you... for old time's sake."

No doubt he would just as soon run Borkul through with his jagged blade.

There were too many goblins in our way for us to get to the humans, but at least now I spied a weapon. A thick branch protruding from the smoldering remains of the campfire was within reach. I made a grab for it. The branch came free with a rain of red cinders, and the doused fire sprang to life again once the air hit the sleeping embers.

Smoke, sparks, flame. The campsite was in chaos. I ignored the charred wood scorching my palm and lashed out at a scurrying shadow. But goblins are quick—especially when they're trying to save their own skins—and the small fighter dodged and parried. I shoved toward him with the hook of my eating knife, but he danced out of reach.

I swung wild with the branch and finally made contact, hitting the goblin with a shower of sparks —

—just as the rest of the goblins made a break for the humans.

8

QUINN

When I found myself surrounded by gargoyles come to life, I'd taken it, initially, for a nightmare.

But they were all too real.

And they were *fast*.

I figured they'd meant to kill us, slaughter us in our sleep. But the lightning-quick swing of a hatchet didn't land on anyone's skull—just the chain tethering Bess to me. Sparks flew...as well as a hunk from the blade. "No good," the thing barked to its companion. It *spoke*.

"Then open it!"

How many of those monsters were there? Hard to say. Not only was it dark, but everything was a shouting, grunting chaos.

"Stay still," the one with the axe snapped at Bess. "You don't want me to slip."

Archie said, "They're on our side—stop struggling!"

As the creature wedged the chipped blade into Bess's collar, I saw it wasn't attacking her—it was trying to free her. But before I could step in and help it by holding the collar still and giving it room to work, I heard one of the other ones complaining, "Why can't those dumb orcs just shackle the wrists like everyone else? We'd take off her hand and be done already."

"She won't last long without her head," the other said. "Though a few of the human sickos would pay to have a go at her before she fell to rot. Even headless."

Clearly *not* on our side.

While Hatchet tried to open Bess's collar, the complainer managed to work loose the spike that was pinning us to the fallen tree. Just as soon as I felt the chain slacken, I reached around Bess and yanked it from the startled beast's hands. The spike flew off into the bushes—a real shame, since I could've used it as a stiletto. But I wasn't empty-handed. I still had the chain.

"Stay close," I told Bess and Archie—because it was bad enough to be surrounded and outnumbered in the dark without tangling myself up in the chained collars. The chain was heavier than my old whip and not nearly as long...but if I connected, I could do some serious damage.

"We only want the female," Hatchet claimed. "Drop the chain and we'll let you live."

I lashed out and cracked it in the kneecap.

It staggered back, hissing. "You'll be sorry!"

Maybe so, but the only thing I'd truly regret was giving up while there was still some fight left in me to make a final stand.

The creatures could likely see better than any of us with their oversized eyes. Between their numbers, their weapons and their eyesight, we were at a major disadvantage—until sparks erupted from the embers of our campfire and the flames leapt back to life.

Those huge eyes were a liability when the fire's hot light washed over us. And while the creatures got their bearings, I wound up and swung again. The end of my chain connected with the complainer's skull with a meaty thump, and he crumpled to the ground. Hatchet pointed at me and barked out an order. "Cut that one free." Meaning, my *head*. If Hatchet stayed out of it, with the complainer down, I was pretty sure I could take on the remaining creature. But then Hatchet raised a bone whistle and blew.

I heard nothing—but, like hunting hounds, the creatures apparently did. The silhouettes of several more gangly figures surged around the campfire from either side. I realized with growing dread that my fleeting notion of making my final stand might have been more of a premonition.

We were surrounded—and I couldn't make any sudden moves without strangling Archie or Bess. What's worse, one of the creatures had a sharpened spear that was easily long enough to outreach my chain, while another wielded a jagged blade that looked fully capable of sawing through my spine.

I swung at the spear, snapped it in two, and whirled around to knock out the one with the blade. But as I did, Hatchet launched himself at me and tossed a handful of dirt in my face. My strike went wide as I blinked frantically to clear my vision. I tried as best I could to fend them off, but didn't connect. Everything was blurred and jumbled, and there were just too many. I'd be damned if I didn't go down fighting... but eventually I was sure to fall.

But then a massive, armored figure burst through the campfire, showering sparks all around. Marok! He landed with a thud between the creature and me, and the jagged blade skittered along the orc's arm, dragging across the armored bracer with a sickening screech. Marok sliced at my attacker with a small, curved knife. With the other hand, he swung a smoldering log, stunning the creature with a solid blow. It was enough of a diversion for me to get in another hit myself, sending Hatchet retreating into the night. Borkul rounded the fire. He pitched a broken hunk of crate and knocked an enemy to its knees. And despite our lack of real weapons, together we somehow drove them off.

Though my relief was premature.

Borkul said, "I saw a good few dozen goblins at the bazaar." So that's what those things were—*goblins*. "They'll be back with reinforcements."

Marok grunted. "Then we'd better get going." He turned to me. "You—horseman. Come yoke the oxen." He tossed me the key to my collar. "And if you think about running off, think again. Goblins don't take kindly to losing. They'll be eager to settle the score for cracking their friend's skull."

Archie had fallen into a spell of coughing, so I handed off the key to Bess so she could free me. She fit it in the collar with trembling fingers, bending her head to mine, and whispered, "What now?"

I recalled the crunch at the end of the one solid hit I'd scored with the chain. "I'd wager he's right. We're better off staying with the orcs."

When the metal collar came off, my neck felt raw and

oddly exposed. With nothing chaining me down—nothing holding me back—if there was any good time to slip away, it was now. But clearly, I was nowhere near the Fortifications. Besides, I couldn't abandon Archie, and especially not Bess. And so headed over to yoke the sleepy oxen. With Marok.

We worked together in silence for several long moments, but as I tightened the yoke, Marok said, "We pushed them hard yesterday. Can they manage?"

I ran my hand over the haunches of the nearest ox, and it responded with a skin flicker and lazy smack of its tail. "It's not ideal," I admitted. "But if we leave them behind, they'll end up on a spit anyhow. We should lighten their load as much as we can. The less they need to pull, the easier they'll have it."

Marok conferred briefly with Borkul, pitched a few crates off the back of the wagon, and rounded us up to go. "We all walk," he announced, then cut a glance at Archie, who was struggling to draw a good breath. "Except that one."

Borkul hoisted Archie into the wagon bed like he was a rag doll. "I doubt the oxen will even notice him."

Anyone who's trained an animal, be it a puppy or a plow horse, knows that every creature has its own personality. But from the moment the orcs stepped through the slaver's tent flap, I'd thought of them as one homogenous race. If not for Borkul's scar, I couldn't even tell them apart. Maybe it was the time we'd spent with them this night. Maybe the bonds created by fighting off a common enemy. But suddenly, I truly saw them as distinct individuals.

Even more baffling...it was Marok, the stern, dour one, who'd been willing to leap through a fire to save me from a goblin's sword.

Borkul grabbed his breastplate from a nearby bush and tugged it over his head. "Should I unshackle the female so she can walk without tripping over the chains?"

Marok glanced at Bess. "Hopefully she's sensible enough not to run off with goblins lurking around." He glanced sharply at me. "Same goes for you, horseman."

"I have a name," I said. "It's Quinn."

"Unless we get going, your name will be *That Dumb Human Who Ended Up as Troll Food Because He Let the Goblins Regroup*."

I held his gaze for a heartbeat, then said, "That's quite a mouthful. How 'bout *Lunch* for short?"

Marok snorted. Evidently, he wasn't entirely devoid of humor after all.

9

MAROK

Even once the lights of the bazaar were well behind us, we kept our pace at a brisk walk. The oxen weren't pleased about it, but the horseman—*Quinn*—said they were healthy enough to endure the forced march.

Though I couldn't say as much for the young human male, who was taxed by merely riding along.

His coughing had a wet, rattling sound to it now. One that didn't bode well.

"Can't we give him something for it?" I asked Borkul.

He shrugged. "The goblins helped themselves to our medicines when they made off with our weapons."

The goblins wouldn't have taken any notice of us whatsoever, had Borkul not brought them back to our camp. But saying as much would gain me nothing except a moment of satisfaction. And I couldn't afford to turn Borkul against me now—not when he was the only one in the clan who would speak to me.

We paused to get our bearings only when we came to the river that marked the edge of our clan's hunting territory. We were still a good three days from home, but at least the land was familiar. I doubted the goblins would follow us this far...though it always pays to watch your back. We'd dealt them some heavy blows—and where payback is concerned, you never know how far someone will go. We forded the river on a sandbar and made our way toward the forest. "We rest in the cover of those trees," I said. "But no fires. We're not making it easier for the goblins to track us down."

As Quinn and I unyoked the oxen, Bokul took stock of what little supplies we had left. "They got most of our food, too. Either that or we tossed it out in our haste to get away. Nothing left but hardtack." He scented the air briefly, and turned over a nearby log. "Good thing there's plenty of wrigglers."

My stomach rumbled in anticipation as Borkul grabbed a handful of big, meaty grubs and crammed them in his mouth—and the female gave off a startling shriek. "Don't worry," Borkul said. "There's enough for everyone."

Quinn said, "We don't, ah.... I've never eaten...." He nodded toward the wrigglers.

"They're good for you," Borkul said through a half-chewed mouthful. "Nice and fresh. Put some meat on those bones."

Quinn considered this. "Different creatures have different diets. You wouldn't feed your oxen meat, for instance. What's good for orcs isn't necessarily good for us."

"More for me." Borkul dug down into the soft, decaying wood to get at the firmest grubs. "But if you've got designs on that hardtack, I'd soak it first, if I were you. Can't see how else your funny little teeth would get through it."

We ate our fill of wrigglers and let the humans figure out how to divvy up the hardtack. The young male, Archie, could barely stop coughing long enough to get it down. We were fortunate that they were so sentimental, so invested in keeping him alive, since without my supply of purchased herbs, I didn't know what to do.

The female, Bess, found a medicinal tree. Its outer bark was soft, even crumbly, and its inner bark was slick with sap. "Normally we would dry it out, then brew a tea." She handed Archie a bit of the slippery, pale inner bark. "Try sucking on this. Maybe it'll help."

After a few moments, his constant hacking slowed to a few occasional coughs.

We decided to leave the humans unchained, since Archie wasn't going anywhere, and shackling them together only left them less able to fend for themselves. But that didn't mean we trusted them. Forging off into the wilderness alone might be stupid. Making off with our oxen and cart, however, would be a reasonable plan.

I took first watch. While Borkul found a flat spot by the bushes and settled down to sleep, the humans huddled together in the cart for warmth.

They were talking low amongst themselves, but their discussion was never about running off. Archie was too weak. And besides, they had no desire to run across more goblins.

Mainly, they whispered about the goblins. None of them had seen one before, though Bess said her parents threatened to feed her and her siblings to goblins if they didn't behave. A sure sign that they had no idea what they were talking about. Goblins might be greedy and treacherous, but of course, they don't *eat* sentient beings.

Maybe they'd mistaken a goblin for a troll.

It wouldn't be the first story to get lost as it passed from mouth to ear.

Later on, when Borkul relieved me, I went to the opposite end of the camp where I could defend us if need be, while keeping out of earshot. I didn't need to hear the thumping of Bess's heart or the shallow, desperate sound of Archie's breath to know that he was getting worse.

In the morning, I woke the horseman and told him to help me with the oxen. Animals prefer the scent of humans... despite the fact that a human is just as likely as an orc to beat or eat them. I wasn't so sure I cared for the smell—the sharp sweat, the strange musk. But I supposed I was getting used to it.

Quinn's muscles strained as we hefted the heavy yoke, but he didn't complain. Despite his soft, pale skin, he seemed sturdy enough. As I ran the peg through the oxbow, he let out a gasp. "Wait—is that blood?"

I glanced at my forearm. "It's nothing."

"That's from the last night, isn't it? When you got between the goblin and me."

"Better see to that goblin wound," Borkul called over. "You know they shit on their weapons so the cuts fester—then dip them in dreamweed so you don't feel it till it's too late."

That was just a rumor...or at least, I hoped it was. "There's no time," I snapped.

But Quinn didn't seem accustomed to taking orders. "What happens if you founder? Dragging Archie along might not slow down the oxen, but you're another story. It'll only take a few minutes to clean it out. Take off that bracer."

We needed to press on. We were barely a day's travel from the bazaar, and in the daylight, our wheel tracks would be hard to miss. This hunting territory was unguarded. It would be at least two more days until we were close enough to the village to stop watching our backs and sleeping with one eye open.

Even so, it was faster to allow the horseman to tend the wound than it would've been to argue. I took off my cuff and let him see to the cut. Though it didn't hurt much, it was still bleeding. I hoped Borkul's predictions about the dreamweed and shit were only talk.

Quinn said, "Your blood is so dark, almost brown."

"Hard to track," I said. "Especially in the forest." Trolls had even better camouflage. Their green blood blended right into the foliage, and in the winter it froze black, impossible to discern from stone.

Quinn's hands were deft as he cleaned the wound and bound it with a poultice of the tree bark we'd been using to treat Archie. Humans have incredibly dextrous fingers, and their close eyesight was just as keen. I hadn't thought we would need to make use of them already, but when I saw the deep gash in my arm, I was glad for those nimble hands.

Once I was wrapped up, we headed deeper into the forest.

If not for the wagon, we could take a more circuitous route to try and evade any potential goblin pursuit. But our shaman, Taruut, had been insistent about bringing back the male with the copper-colored hair—and the handprint on the human's cheek had sealed the deal. And so, unless we wanted to carry Archie all the way back to the borders of the Red Hand Clan, we'd need to stick to the main path.

The off ox actually nuzzled Quinn when we got back on the road. That beast was so stubborn the best I'd ever hoped for from him was to move off my foot—and only if I gave him a good shove. I'd been leery of going all this way to obtain some humans. The shaman had claimed what we found under the slaver's tent would be the key to everything. But Taruut said many things. These days, most of them were scarcely even coherent.

Bess had been an obvious choice. She was young and hardy, and the embroidery on her tunic was filthy from her time in the cage, but it had been done with skill. From nets to ropes—maybe even chainmail—her skills would be in high demand.

Quinn, I'd nearly passed over. He was obviously stronger than the others, and confident, too. The sort of behavior you'd want in a clanmate, but never a slave. Humans were bad enough at following their own authorities, let alone that of an orcish master. It had been risky to buy him. He could have been lying about his training, after all. But one look at him caring for the oxen and it was obvious he was exactly who he'd claimed to be.

"Step lively," Borkul told the humans. "We're too close to the river for my liking."

"Why's that a problem?" Quinn asked.

A captain could cut out his soldier's tongue for challenging his authority like that—but this wasn't war. And Borkul was only amused by the human's audacity. "It's a problem because the Lame Stag River has been so fickle lately. Dwindling to a stream of piss in the dry season. Swelling like a pregnant doe with the rains. And meandering around like a drunkard who can't hold his ale. It wouldn't much matter...

if it weren't the border between us and our 'friendly' neighbors across the bank."

"The Stag has always shifted," I told them, "But never too far. Last spring, though, it redrew itself, curving like a snake, cutting well into Red Hand territory on one curve, and the lands of the Two Swords Clan with the other."

Borkul said, "It was a fair enough exchange. Until the great storm changed its course again and created an island right smack in the middle. Now the clans are at war over a strip of land—land that'll probably choose its own side the next time the rains are low."

He didn't go so far as to say our chieftain was wrong to fight...though I doubt he would have spoken so freely within earshot of our village.

And as for me...I dared say nothing at all. I was lucky the chieftain hadn't exiled me—or worse—after my last command went so horribly wrong.

I wouldn't have consulted with the senile shaman—would never have been on this wild goose chase for a human with hair like copper—if not for the decimation of my troop. I was still unconvinced these humans would be my salvation.

But if my clan rode in on warhorses...not only would the Two Swords Clan stop harrying us.

They'd surrender.

And a conflict simmering for a decade would finally be over.

We pushed ourselves as fast as Quinn deemed the oxen could go. When nightfall came, I was fairly sure the goblins hadn't followed. Goblins are vindictive, yes. But their legs are short, and they're notoriously lazy. Besides, we would've heard their chatter by now.

On the off-chance that those goblins were stealthier and more persistent than I thought, I didn't want to risk a fire. But Bess was shivering, Archie looked like death, and even the strong horseman was chafing his hands together. "A small fire," I allowed. "But make sure the wood is good and dry so we don't send up a giant, billowing signal."

I brushed against Quinn when we unyoked the oxen, and his hand came away stained with blood—rich red-brown blood like the clay of the riverbank. Orcish blood.

"Let me see your arm," he demanded, and I was too curious myself to make him check his tone. "The bindings are still tight. It's hardly bled through at all. Then where...?" He pointed with a gasp at my flank. "Marok—you're really hurt."

10

QUINN

Hard to say if Marok couldn't feel the wound in his side thanks to the dreamweed...or if it was just his habit to minimize his injuries. But now that I'd spotted the blood—a rust-brown that blended right in with the leather straps on his armor—I realized he'd taken a nasty hit.

I knew plenty about minimizing. Training animals required projecting an outward calm, no matter the inner turmoil. Rather than make a fuss over his injury, I simply said, "Your wound will only slow us down if it festers. Take off your armor so I can treat it."

Clearly, Marok was no stallion. Yet he responded to my tone nonetheless.

Archie was dozing fitfully in the wagon and Bess had gone off with Borkul to forage while he hunted small game, which left Marok and me alone. As the orc peeled off his armor, I spotted a blade strapped to his thigh. A smallish thing about as long as my outstretched hand. It was curved, not made for stabbing, but for slashing. One quick stroke across the neck was all it would take for me to make my escape.

But I recognized that weapon. He'd been wielding it when he leapt through the fire to come between me and the goblin attackers...and what kind of ass would I be if I used the blade he'd defended me with to cut his throat?

It may have been a trick of the firelight, but when Marok lifted the chest plate over his head, the way the light played over his torso, he looked very nearly human. Huge, yes. Ridiculously muscular? No doubt. The thing was, I'd always had a yen for the big guys. The stonecutters and bodyguards, the blacksmiths and the porters.

And Marok's body put even the best of them to shame.

Maybe I'd absorbed some of that dreamweed myself—because I should no more admire the physique of an orc than take a fancy to one of the oxen.

And yet, the chiseled bands of sinew framing his pelvis didn't exactly call the oxen to mind.

Marok set the armor aside and squatted on his haunches, treating me to a look of bland patience. The time to snatch his knife had come and gone. Instead of disappointment, though, what I felt was mainly...relief.

The medicinal bark we'd harvested was dry and leathery now, so I soaked it in clean water while I swabbed the blood from the wound in his side to gauge how bad it was. Fresh blood was still oozing from the cut. I probed gently and my fingers came away wet, stained coppery brown. Marok didn't make a sound, didn't even flinch.

"It's deep," I told him.

"Good thing it's still bleeding, then. All the better to flush out the goblin shit."

Maybe so. "I'll wrap the poultice lightly." I pressed the moistened bark to the wound. "Here, hold it while I tie off the bandage."

Marok's huge hand dwarfed mine as he put it against the wet bundle. His fingers were cool and calloused where they brushed against the side of my hand.

Stop it, I told myself as I circled his body with a strip of fabric. *He's just a talking beast—of course, you're not turned on.* But the act of wrapping bandages around his torso was telling my baser instincts otherwise. His waist was trim and lean, and even so, I could barely get my arms around him. And that pressed my cheek against the sharply cut muscles of his chest.

I tied off the bandage and stepped back quickly...but as I did, I found the orc watching me with a peculiar look in his eyes, head tilted, nostrils flaring as he whiffed the air.

I dusted my hands together and brusquely said, "You should get some rest."

He held my gaze for half a heartbeat, then began strapping on his armor without a word.

That night, as I curled up by the fire with a bellyful of fresh rabbit, I tried my best not to dwell on what had taken place between Marok and me. I was being a fool...which I supposed was nothing new. But usually my foolishness had more to do with my own self-importance and less to do with men.

Over the course of my life, I was always overstepping my bounds. Contradicting my teachers. Disagreeing with my superiors. Rubbing potential employers wrong. I couldn't seem to grasp diplomacy, to restrain myself from speaking up when I knew damn well I was right. So, feigning humility was a skill I'd never quite mastered.

But men? Men were easy.

Some men would rather cut off their own dick than let another man suck it, while others were happy to oblige—and might even return the favor...so long as no one found out. Reading a man is like reading an untrained steed. Stance, eye contact, overall demeanor. All of it adds up to a message. And knowing how to interpret that message had got me pretty far with my own hide intact.

Though, considering how badly I'd misjudged the last man to grace my bed, maybe not.

The blacksmith's apprentice aside, I did know how to read men. But while Marok might look like a man, I couldn't let myself forget he was very much not a man at all...but an orc.

11

MAROK

The humans bedded down close to the fire while I squatted by the bushes, listening for the footfalls of anything that shouldn't be there. Normally, I'd be scenting the air, too. But the smell of the humans was blotting out everything else.

Compared to other scents—the oxen team, or the goblins and their cloying sandflower—their smells weren't overbearing. More like...confusing. Because when the horseman put his arms around me, I got a noseful of something that smelled like arousal. So it was clear I knew nothing at all about how humans were supposed to smell.

Most likely I was thrown by the way the horseman had felt when he pressed up against me. He was only binding the wound. But I hadn't been touched by anyone since I lost Akala. It took me by surprise, was all. The feel of another body. Even for a moment.

Once Borkul banked the fire, he ambled over and squatted down beside me, dusting the ash from his hands. "There's cautious, Marok, and then there's paranoid. You don't need to keep watch. Those goblins are far behind us."

"The humans might still turn on us."

"The young one is half dead. The female doesn't have the strength to even break skin. And the horseman, well...." His eyes danced with mischief. "I think he's sweet on you."

I snorted. "You're confusing sweet with sweat."

"Still, no one would blame you for sampling him."

"Think about it, Borkul. If you brought home the prize boar of the first spring hunting expedition, would you take a bite out of it before you lay it at Ul-Rott's feet? Never. Quinn is for the chieftain."

"For the chieftain's *stable*. Not his bed."

Maybe so. Time was, I might be brazen enough to embrace that distinction and sample more of the human's scent for myself. But after my attempt to claim the new island went so horribly wrong, I'd better not screw things up. Not again.

Borkul picked his teeth with a twig. "If you're not gonna bed him, then chain him up and get yourself some shut-eye."

While Borkul might not have acted concerned about the potential for the humans to slay us in our sleep, I noted he did bed down well on the opposite side of the fire, with a scattering of dried leaves around him to sound an alert should anything sneak up. As the others slept, I did the same, clearing just enough space for my body, surrounding it with noisy dead twigs and bark.

A few of those twigs were not twigs at all, but old bones.

Hardly a surprise to find bones in the forest. The world may well grow from a garden of death. But it was the marks on the bones that disturbed me. The gouge of sharp eyeteeth was not surprising, either. Many creatures, from predators to scavengers, would leave that sort of mark. But the twin tracks of paired fangs—four up top, four on the bottom— could only be made by trolls.

At least it wasn't fresh. And many would say it was a good omen to come across the stale path of a wandering troll. The horrid beasts are territorial—which usually makes them easy to avoid. True, they'll build their nests in places where prey wanders by, alongside a trail or tucked beneath a bridge. But when folks start disappearing, anyone with half a brain will figure out they should find a different route.

But a wandering troll—one driven out from the nest they'd claimed—was far more dangerous. Because a wandering troll could turn up anywhere.

I shuddered and chucked the bone into the bushes. None of the humans stirred. Neither did Borkul. I needed sleep, but could I really allow myself the comfort when my heart-brother was so vulnerable? With a sigh, I settled into a vigilant crouch to watch over my camp. Occasionally I prodded at the wound in my side to see if the dreamweed was wearing off. And occasionally I glanced at Quinn's sleeping form.

It would be easy to deny it was arousal I'd scented on him... had Borkul not noticed it, too.

I supposed I should consider myself lucky there was no telltale scent to loneliness.

12

QUINN

The next morning, I checked Marok's wound. It was obvious that between the flickering firelight and the dark of night, my eyes had been playing tricks on me. By the light of day, the orc looked nothing like a man. His hide was a mottled grayish green, and his limbs were so thick with muscle it was a wonder he could even move. "Does it hurt?" I asked as I peeled off the poultice.

His only answer was a noncommittal grunt.

I pressed the backs of my fingers gently to his side. The cut was still bleeding sluggishly, but at least the skin around it wasn't hot or inflamed.

"Will I live?" he asked.

And again I was caught off-guard by the dryness of his humor.

Given that the wound hadn't closed, he would have been

better off leaving off his armor, but he was no more likely to go without it than to ride in the back of the wagon with Archie. If not for the thin trickle of brownish blood running down his side, I wouldn't have even known he was injured.

But Archie was another story.

He wasn't coughing, not anymore, but he shivered violently despite the warmth of the day. The orcs conferred briefly, then told Bess to keep watch on him while we traveled, and hoisted her into the wagon beside him. "We should grant him a mercy," I heard Borkul say.

Marok shook his head. "He's the whole reason we made this journey. If he wants to keep struggling like this, we let him."

I wasn't sure if they knew I was listening…or maybe it was more that they didn't care. I might not be in irons, but regardless, I was still a captive. These were orc woods. If I ran, I'd be just as likely to run *away* from the Fortifications as toward them. Besides, I'd be as easy for them to track down as a lame doe.

"You didn't need to come," Marok said to the other orc after a long silence. "But you did. When no one else stood by me…you did."

Borkul whacked him on the shoulder with a blow that would've sent me sprawling. "Bah, what are heart-brothers for?"

Without goblins on our tails and no need to lighten the load, we could have all ridden. But I preferred to lead the oxen from the ground—and Marok took up his position at the opposite side of the team. Borkul was happy enough to ride, though, and he snoozed from the driver's bench, head lolling.

We walked in silence for ages. Evidently, orcs aren't much for chitchat. But eventually, my curiosity got the better of me. "Why Archie?" I asked.

Marok glanced across the team and briefly met my eye. "It was foretold."

Not sure what reason I'd been expecting...but it certainly wasn't that. "How?"

He answered my question with a question. "Does your village have a shaman?"

I came from a city, not a village. And a *witch doctor*? "Of course not."

"Then you wouldn't understand."

"So...explain it to me."

"You ask too many questions. It's not our way—and the chieftain won't indulge your human curiosity for long. If you're smart, you'll learn to do what you're told and keep your mouth shut."

And that, apparently, was all he was willing to say about it.

We trudged along in silence, stopping only to finish off what was left of the hardtack and jerky. The trail joined with another, and grew wider and more deeply rutted as we neared the orc village. The sun was lowering and the nighttime cold was settling in. I knew I could hardly expect a featherbed and glass of wine. But it was obvious the orcs were invested enough in keeping us alive to feed us, so I was looking forward to a meal and a warm fire.

...and was greeted by a rotten head on a stake.

It wasn't human—at least, I didn't think so, but it was so decomposed, it was really hard to tell. The pole was a good five or six hands taller than me, tufted with garish, brightly colored feathers around the neck so you couldn't possibly miss it. The scalp had peeled open, exposing the white curve of a skull. The eyes were long gone, pecked out by scavenging crows, no doubt.

Marok took no notice of the grisly head whatsoever, and Borkul was still dozing in his seat. I was burning to ask about it, but figured I'd only piss the orcs off.

Still...when I saw the second head, I couldn't stop myself from asking.

"What about the...y'know...?" Marok glanced at me and said nothing. I sighed. "The heads?"

"We mark our borders with a warning to our enemies. That one was a mongrel who tried to break into our armory. The green feathers mark him as a thief. When another thief sees it, he'll know better than to target the Clan of the Red Hand."

Up until now, I'd only heard the term *mongrel* used in regard to a dog. But the head on the pole was unlike any dog I'd ever seen. The skin color was nothing to go by, an ashen, greenish black. The skull shape didn't seem quite as flat as a goblin's or as tall as an orc's. Frankly, he looked a bit like the blacksmith's uglier son, though I was sure he'd never set foot beyond the Fortifications' walls. The one remaining ear, I saw, was slightly pointed.

"Who are the mongrels?"

"Not who—what. Creatures that are neither one thing nor the other. That one had some goblin in him, I'd wager. Maybe some troll, too."

By the time we came upon the next warning head, I was still stuck on the notion that trolls and goblins were capable of producing viable offspring together. "A goblin can mate with a troll?"

"Only a stupid one who doesn't value its own head," he chortled. "Trolls aren't known for their romantic nature." He glanced at me over the team. "How are you so sure of yourself when you don't know anything?"

Good question. "Maybe it's in your best interest to educate me so I don't end up asking something stupid and making you look bad."

He shook his head ruefully...but didn't disagree.

I said, "I'm not entirely hopeless—I know that a dog can hump a cat all it wants, but that doesn't mean there's a litter of puppycats on the way."

"Animals are animals. Sentient races are men. Why some beings can think and others not, who's to say? Maybe, long ago, we who know ourselves were all the same." Fascinating. Back at the bazaar, maybe there hadn't been a dozen different monstrous races after all, but the byproducts of the mixing and mingling of just a few. "You're not as advanced as orcs, of course." He gave his ox a pat. "But you're not animals, either."

I knew I wasn't supposed to ask any questions—but I was getting much more of an education than I'd bargained for.

"Now, that one there..." he pointed up at a ghastly male head, eyeless, half-crushed, beard crusted with dried blood. "Pretty sure he's all human."

I counted twenty stakes in all—and that was only on the particular path we were traveling on to the orc village.

Given that the path was lined with heads, I expected to find something horrific at the end. But instead, there was just a wall of hardened timber, logs sharpened at the top, stretching off into the trees on one side, and out toward a sheltering bluff on the other. Nothing like the stone Fortifications, obviously. But though it was primitive, I didn't doubt it was effective.

As we approached, a pair of armored orcs met us—a male and a female. The female's armor fitted the curves of her trim waist and lush hips in a way that suggested she hadn't just thrown on something designed for a man...which meant it wasn't unusual for the women here to have things like armor. She wore her dark hair longer than the men did, pulled back and plaited. She wasn't much taller than me, but if I challenged her to an arm wrestling match, no doubt she'd put me through the table. Both orcs had the greenish skin and the broad, muscular build of Marok and Borkul, but each one's features were totally distinct.

I can tell them all apart now, I realized.

If the guards were surprised to find their clan members traveling with humans, they didn't show it. Actually, they strode right past Marok and me to talk to Borkul.

In greeting, both guards thumped their chest plates and said, "Praise Ul-Rott."

"My sword is his," Borkul replied easily. "Tell me, has your brother made any headway with his archery since I left?"

The male guard smirked. "Hardly. Unless you count shooting over the targets as a win. What have you brought back with you?"

"Three humans."

The guard sniffed, nostrils flaring. "No goblins?"

"Naw—we left those right where we found 'em."

Never mind that the guards could smell goblin on us at all. But three days later? Impressive—and more than a bit daunting. I must have been thinking that once I got my bearings, I could help myself to some supplies, slip off, and find my way back to the Fortifications. Now, though, I saw that if I ever got past the barricades, an orc could track me down faster than a bloodhound.

The female guard rounded the wagon and peered inside. "Just the three humans?"

"That's it," Borkul assured her.

"Okay, then—you're cleared to enter."

"Praise Ul-Rott," Borkul murmured, and Marok tugged the yoke, nudging the team toward the gate.

Travelers were challenged all the time on their way into the Fortifications, so that was nothing new. But something about the whole exchange still struck me as odd. On the road, Marok had seemed to be the one calling the shots. And yet, at the gate…. "Why didn't the guards talk to you?"

"What did I say about asking questions?" he huffed. "We're not out in the woods anymore. In the chieftain's lodge, if you want to keep your tongue, you shut your damn mouth."

I sensed that he was nowhere near as worried about my tongue as he claimed to be. More likely, he didn't want to answer the question.

Given the heads, I was expecting to find some barbaric, freakish tableau inside the gates. But the village was not only devoid of random dismembered body parts—it was surprisingly neat. The structures were all made of wood, but they were nothing like the filthy scrap wood shantytowns in the poor districts of the Fortifications.

The dirt streets of the shantytowns ran with muck, with all the residents flinging their chamber pots out the doors with no concern for where the waste landed. Feral dogs roamed the winding alleyways hunting for rats. And the buildings were stacked so close together, most of them sharing at least one wall, that when someone knocked over a candle, half the neighborhood went up.

The orc village was built with exacting care. Each building was the same size, laid out to a precise grid. And each wall was constructed from stripped logs clearly chosen for their uniformity. Not only were the streets laid with cobblestones...there wasn't a single emptied chamber pot to be found.

We passed a few dozen small homes and made our way deeper into the village. The buildings here were bigger—communal spaces. Smoke rose from both clay ovens and a smithy's forge. Orcs hauled buckets from a well. A wheelwright banged some spokes into place. Normal things. Yet not normal at all, because everyone worked with a notable sense of purpose—and a profound air of discipline.

There was no haggling, no gambling, no shifty beggar lingering in the shadows hoping to relieve someone of their purse. No doubt I had questions. But even if I were dumb enough to voice them after being repeatedly warned to keep my mouth shut, I couldn't have quite articulated what my question was.

We followed the cobblestone road to the center of the village, where a group of orcs waiting to greet us stood around a bonfire. A colorful canopy had been erected beside it—nothing at all like the silks in the Fortification fairgrounds, but just as well made. Beneath the canopy, elaborately decked out in feathers and carved bones, a figure sprawled on a sedan chair. This orc, I realized, was the first one I'd seen sitting down...though I didn't think it was due to his station. As we neared, I saw he was not simply old—he was ancient.

He sat with his eyes closed. As we approached, he tilted

his head back and sniffed the air, lips parted to let the scent play over his tongue. "You've brought the human," he said. "No...you've got more than one."

He opened his eyes, and I saw they were the blind, pale, milky green of an overboiled egg.

"Kneel," Marok told me as he folded to one knee. I did the same as Borkul hopped down from the wagon and joined us on the hard cobblestone. Eyes downcast, he told the old man, "Taruut the Wise...we are unworthy of your blessing."

I'd presumed the blind orc was their chieftain, so I was surprised when he waved a negligent hand and said, "My blessing means nothing. I'm just an old shaman who's over-stayed his time in the world."

Borkul said, "You honor us with your attention."

"You brought me the human boy, did you not?" He gave a dry chuckle. "I'd hardly turn you away."

Four strong orcs stood around the shaman, all decorated with feathers, wearing streaks of white paint on each cheek. With a wave of their master's hand, they all moved as one to hoist his litter. "Bring me to him," the shaman said, and without a verbal cue of any sort, somehow they knew exactly which way to walk.

They rounded the wagon and stood patiently, holding the orc and his bulky litter waist-high, so he was level with the wooden platform. The shaman sniffed again. Borkul shoved me in the shoulder and whispered, "Don't stare." I quickly followed his example and planted my eyes front and center.

"Well, the boy's pretty far gone, isn't he?" the shaman asked no one in particular. "I suppose I don't have much time."

For what?

Even I knew better than to ask.

"And his hair?" the shaman prompted.

Borkul said, "As you foretold. Bright like a copper penny."

"Good. And don't worry, Marok—yes, I know you're there, even if you haven't dared open your mouth. I'll put in a good word for you with Ul-Rott."

Marok finally spoke. "But what about the other humans?"

"Bah, I have no time for them now, what with the boy half-dead. Until I get around to their purification, you're stuck with them yourself."

13

MAROK

Quinn had questions. Big surprise. I could see it in his eyes—but somehow he managed to hold his tongue. I bid Borkul goodbye, left the wagon at the wainwright's, and chained the two humans together again so they couldn't do anything stupid. Any humans I'd previously come across—the humans at the bazaar, the itinerant traders—seemed to know something about the world. But these two came from some far-flung place where no one had taught them much about anything.

I'd never had to deal with anyone so ignorant. They were worse than babies. At least babies couldn't stab you in your sleep—not with enough force to give you more than a flesh wound, anyhow.

I marched them back to my quarters. It was the same home I'd shared with Akala. A family home—too big for one person. We hadn't borne children. Not yet. We always thought there'd be plenty of time.

How wrong we were.

Most orcs would not want unpurified strangers in their homes. Who knows what sort of ill omens they might track in? For me, though, it made no difference. Things couldn't get much worse. First, losing Akala...then, losing the respect of the whole clan. I supposed the Red Hand could always stop shunning me and toss me out altogether. But maybe that would be a relief.

"If you require a soft bed," I announced, "I have none."

The female, Bess, sniffled. Her scent went saline.

"What's wrong?" I demanded.

Quinn squared his shoulders. "She's been through a lot. We both have. You don't need to yell."

This was their idea of yelling? They hadn't heard me command threescore orcish warriors. "You should be grateful—I'm telling you how things are. *Someone* has to." I gestured at my winter coverings. "Use the furs on that shelf if you're too delicate to sleep on the floor."

Quinn reached for a particular bearskin, and I said, "Not that one. Any of the others."

"It'll be okay," I heard him murmur to Bess, who was now fully weeping. Again.

How such soft creatures ever survived in this world, I'd never understand. My home was spacious, three full rooms, but it was clear I couldn't leave the humans to their own devices. I'd need to keep my eye on them.

"Are the collars really necessary?" Quinn asked.

"Are they?" I countered.

His shoulders slumped. Just a bit. "Listen—there are more

orcs than I can count between here and the forest, not to mention a well-guarded wall twice as tall as me."

"Don't forget the trolls," Bess whispered.

"We're not going anywhere. It's just a little hard to sleep with an iron band around your neck."

I dug out the key from a pouch at my belt and tossed it at his feet. "If you think you can talk your way past those guards, think again. They don't negotiate. They kill. They'd slay you without thinking twice."

"Understood," Quinn said, unlocking Bess's collar.

She sank to the floor and curled up on her side, trying to make herself as small and inconspicuous as possible.

Truly, it was a wonder they weren't all dead by now.

Once they were both unchained, Quinn set to work padding the floor with my furs. My collection was impressive, though I couldn't take any credit for it. Akala was the one always eager to go hunting. Whenever we could steal off alone, we'd head for the woods. Sometimes we'd intend to track down prey and end up coupling. Sometimes a fresh trail piqued our curiosity and we'd leave the sex for later. Usually, we made time for both.

And now the humans were rubbing their scent all over the pelts we'd collected.

She would have found this amusing, I think. My wife took things in stride.

"Where is the chamber pot?" I heard Bess whisper.

Akala help me. "What kind of animals do you think we are?" I said. "We don't shit in the house. You'll use the latrine like a civilized person. Come on." I nodded toward the door. "Let's go."

It was a bit of a walk to get to the latrines—more evidence

of the status I used to enjoy. A mongrel slave keeps things covered, but even so, the smell reached us long before the pits were in sight.

Heads turned as I strode up the street, herding along two humans. But no one asked. Even the ones I'd played soldier with when we were young boys.

The female seemed perplexed by the holes in the ground. I gestured for the mongrel. He was part dwarf, part goblin—and missing a hand, thanks to his attempt to steal our winter provisions. Lucky for him he'd been unarmed at the time. Otherwise, it would have cost him his life. He bowed and bobbed as he shuffled over, eyes averted. Orcs might shun me now, but years of deference had been beaten into the mongrel. "Explain the latrines," I told him. "And make sure the humans behave."

When they were through relieving themselves, Quinn *still* had questions, I could tell.

His curiosity would be his undoing.

I marched them again to my quarters and slammed the door behind us. Bess flinched. Quinn cocked an eyebrow. "All right," I said. "Since you don't know even the most basic things, I'll start at the beginning. Don't throw your crap in the street—we're not monkeys flinging shit. You'll be expected to contribute. Everyone contributes to earn their place in the clan. Don't ask questions—it would be taken as a challenge. Look someone in the eye when you're talking to them, but don't stare, not unless you want a fight."

"But what about the shaman?" Quinn asked.

"Of course you don't make eye contact with the shaman. Or the chieftain, either. They're not just orcs. They're leaders. You treat them with respect, or you have it beaten into you."

"What if my version of respect is different from an orc's?"

I bit back a sigh. He'd be lucky to last the week.

"Respect means effort," I said. "Respect means self-sacrifice. Above all, respect means obedience."

"And looking someone in the eye. But not for too long... and not if they're a leader."

"Exactly."

"Allrighty, then. No problem."

I headed toward my sleeping chamber, but paused at the door, curious now. "Were there no leaders among your humans?"

Bess had rolled up in the furs, feigning sleep, but her heartbeat was too rapid for slumber. She was smart to watch and listen. Quinn, though, was pawing through my shelves. "Sure, there were officials, but I didn't really answer to any of them directly. Most folks in my line of work don't have to deal with the mayor, or the constables, or anyone involved with the government."

"Then who would you answer to?"

He shrugged. "My employer, I suppose. It's different inside the Fortifications."

Indeed.

Quinn dropped a doeskin on the floor and folded onto it—cross-legged, like a child. "What are you doing?" I snapped.

He stared at me for an insolent beat. "Sitting down?"

"How are you even alive?" I squatted beside him. "This is how a grown man sits. By the time you got to your feet, there'd be a blade through your skull."

"Was someone planning to attack me in your house?" he said, eyes dancing. I glared. "Okay...point taken." He got his feet under him. "This isn't exactly comfy on the knees."

"You get used to it."

After a few moments, he stood, wincing slightly, and shook out his legs. "We should probably take a look at that stab wound before you go to sleep."

The dreamweed had worn off a while ago. I could feel the heat of the injury every time I moved. "If you try anything stupid—" I warned.

"A thousand pissed-off orcs will use me for target practice. Listen, I might not know where to look or how to sit, but I promise, I'm not an entirely lost cause."

He lit a lantern—at least he knew how to use a flint—and helped me lift my breastplate over my head. Something fluttered in my gut at the anticipation of him circling my waist with his arms again. But removing the dressings was not the same as putting them on. He simply untied the knot and pulled them off, leaving me oddly disappointed.

When he pressed cool, smooth fingers to the cut's ragged edge, it wasn't painful...it was soothing.

"Not to ask too many questions...but is there anything here I can treat this with?"

"I'll allow it," I said, and showed him where I kept my herbs and tinctures.

He sniffed one, then another. "The barkberries," I said. "No, the other pouch. Rub them fine and dust it over the wound."

He poured a handful into a bowl and began breaking up the dried fruits. "Wow, this packs a punch," he said, flicking a scrap out of a hangnail.

"It does sting. But it's better than an infection."

Quinn was unfamiliar with our customs, but his mind

was quick. He knew some of my herbs, though by different names. And his touch was somehow both gentle and sure. "Normally, I'd stitch this up," he said. "But it's *still* bleeding, three days in. Almost like your body is trying to.... Wait. Hold up that lantern."

As I raised it over his head, I realized that if Quinn really wanted to seize the opportunity, this would be the perfect time to disable me. You don't need a weapon to take advantage of an injury. He could take me down with something as harmless as a spoon if he jammed it in there hard enough.

There was a short, sharp pain....

"Look," he breathed, holding up a small shard of rusted metal, slick with my blood. "That goblin left you a souvenir."

If whatever the goblin had coated his blade with didn't fester inside me, the hunk of metal would. "Good," I said simply. "Now the barkberries."

As Quinn worked, treating the deep wound, I rolled the small shard between my forefinger and thumb. An orcish healer would not have seen it. Too small. And they wouldn't have felt it, either. Our skin is too thick. Only a human has such a fine, deft touch. Or a dwarf—but you'd never find one outside their mountain. And if you do, chances are, they're drunk.

His fingers had been beneath my skin—if only for a moment. To bring me to my knees, all he'd had to do was cram them in. No doubt he was fully aware of the opportunity. But he hadn't taken advantage of it.

Barkberries are astringent, but they don't give off much of a smell. They did nothing to conceal the lingering traces of the human scent his nearness had left on me.

Nor did they obliterate the way he picked up my own

scent by being in my house and handling my things. And my blood.

"I could bind the wound again," he said, "but given how spotless this place is, I'd take the opportunity to let it air out."

I agreed. Though I was disappointed that I wouldn't feel his arms around me.

Hmph. I'd been too long without coupling if I was hungry to slake my want on a human.

Quinn washed at the basin to clean the blood and bark from his hands, but instead of rinsing away my scent, the water just softened it and drove it deeper, mingling it with his. It was a peculiar smell, this combination of orc and human. Though, I supposed, not unpleasant.

No. He belonged to the chieftain, and once he was purified, I'd be rid of him. I'd gone an entire turning of the season without sex. I could go another night.

He peeled off his shirt to wash away the dust of our travels, and the scent of his musk welled up around me. What was merely tolerable before was now a stark enticement.

Quinn took down a soft sheepskin from the shelf and pulled it around his shoulders. Our scents melded and merged.

I considered…. If I was careful not to spill directly on him, Ul-Rott might never know it was anything more than the smell of my house on the human. Maybe. Maybe not. I ignored the way my want was pooling low in my belly, creeping down to my groin.

"So…sleeping," he said. "Am I allowed to lie down? Or is the orcish way to do it standing up, with one eye open?"

"You talk too much." I dragged a heavy cabinet in front of the outer door just in case either of them tried getting away despite my warnings, then grabbed the bearskin from the highest shelf.

My sleeping chamber was dark, which made its familiar scents wrap themselves around me. It used to smell like Akala and me...but not anymore. Not for many moons past. The bearskin, though...it had been her favorite. I stretched out in my usual spot and brought the pelt to my face, searching for any remaining traces of my wife. But I couldn't be sure if I actually scented her...or if it was only my imagination.

14

QUINN

I'd love to think I could truly manage to sleep with one eye open—but the orc's home was not only scrupulously clean, but warm and quiet. Back in the Fortifications, I was used to the sounds of my neighbors carousing. But here, carousing—like sitting cross-legged—must not have been allowed.

Maybe there was no mattress, but Marok had more pelts than a fur trader. The bed I made for myself was more lavish than any mattress I could afford, and before I knew it, I was deeply asleep.

"Quinn?"

Daylight streamed through the high, narrow windows as Bess shook me awake. I was startled, disoriented, duped by the soft furs into thinking I'd fallen asleep in some wealthy man's bed and not an orc settlement.

I rolled over and gave Bess a reassuring smile. Her eyes

were red-rimmed and her cheeks were pale, but at least she'd stopped crying. She whispered, "Do you think the monster would notice if I washed up a little?"

I suspected our captor noticed everything. "Maybe. But he didn't mind when I did."

"That's different. You're a man. Men can do as they please."

I thought back to the guards at the gate. That female orc didn't seem like she'd take any guff. "Marok has treated us fairly so far. Even if you were to step out of line, claim human ignorance and you'll get away with a stern warning."

Bess hurried to the basin and splashed herself off, almost surreptitiously, like she was sure she'd be chastised. She was filthy, both from her time in the slaver's tent and on the road, and a quick wipe would hardly do much to help.

She was quick to come back to our nest of furs and settle in, positioning herself so that I was between her and the orc in the other room.

"At least they treat us better than the slavers," I said, trying to cheer her up.

"Better than a lot of places I've been," she said with a humorless laugh. "Better than my uncle, after my parents died. He beat me whenever he took to drink. And it's better than wandering around the Wastelands half-dead, after the household he sold me to did this—" she grabbed a fistful of her shorn hair for emphasis, "and threw me out without a thing to my name."

Guess she hadn't sold it for a wig after all. "Why would anyone do something like that?"

"Normally, I tended the children. Taught them their stitching, their letters, their prayers. But the family was hosting a big party, a fancy thing for their wealthier relatives from across town. They brought me out front with the parlor maids to make their staff look bigger. That was when I caught the master's eye."

"You don't need to spell it out," I said. "I've worked for a wealthy household or two myself. But...why your hair?"

"His wife claimed I stole a silver hairbrush. Said it was a fitting punishment."

And now Bess was there beside me in an orcish village. I somehow doubted the orcs needed her to wipe their children's snotty noses and tuck them into bed. Especially since they didn't *have* beds.

Though they didn't have any horses that I could see, either. So who's to say what they wanted with either of us? Back when the goblins attacked us by the fire, Borkul seemed awfully familiar with them. Not just the female goblin, either. So, it seemed orcs weren't as uptight about their conquests as the men in the Fortifications could be. In terms of both gender...and species.

Which meant we shouldn't get too comfortable, because the worst might very well be yet to come.

Even if I did get a thrill from slipping my arms around Marok.

I took a look around, hoping to gain some insight into him. His home was unlike anywhere I'd ever been, both crammed full of things, yet somehow austere. There were chests and shelves, baskets and bureaus, all of them brimming with stuff. Lots of it was quite valuable, or at the very least, useful. But not a single damn place to sit, unless you wanted to crouch on the wooden slats of the floor—a floor that was so scrupulously clean that the only grit on it was whatever barkberry dust had fallen when I was treating his wound.

If I touched Marok's stuff, I suspected, he'd know—so I didn't handle so much as a candlestick. Only looked. The home had no kitchen, though there was a small hearth with a kettle, and a rack of wine jugs and wooden cups in the corner. In addition to that, there was clothing and armor and a spread of dried herbs and twigs that put my local apothecary to shame. And, of course, the furs. So many pelts.

And that was just his main room.

I might be confident, but I'm not stupid. Did I wonder about Marok's sleeping chambers? Of course. Most working folks I knew didn't even have a room all to themselves, let alone a separate bedroom. The nobility or the ultra-wealthy merchants could afford all that space, in their mansions with their parlors and libraries and greenhouses and stables, while the rest of us were lucky to share a room. But while I didn't dare snoop through Marok's bedchamber, I did keep watch on the door from the corner of my eye...and I was looking when the sleeping orc suddenly stood up in a single, fluid motion.

Maybe they *had* mastered the trick of sleeping with one eye open, after all.

He planted himself in the doorway and scanned the room. "I trust no one has shit in the house while I slept," he said dryly.

Bess went pale.

"He's kidding," I told her. If either of us *had*, he'd probably be able to smell it from the other side of the village.

He told us to put away the furs—then made us fold and re-fold them until we'd arranged them to his satisfaction. He wasn't threatening, exactly. More like...stern. And clearly accustomed to giving orders.

Which made the way the gate guards had ignored him even more curious.

Once everything was put away, swept, and polished, he marched us out to the latrines, then over to a huge communal building of post and wattle with a big hearth at the center. Inside, orcs squatted here and there, drinking from steaming bowls.

Don't stare, I reminded myself.

While they seemed pretty curious about us, when they noticed we were with Marok, they immediately went back to their food as if we weren't even there. Marok walked us over to a stack of clay bowls and gestured for us each to take one. "One dip only. Once you've earned your keep, maybe you can have seconds."

I wasn't sure what, exactly, was bubbling away in the huge stewpot—but it smelled like heaven. It had been so long since I'd had a hot meal, I didn't even care what it was. Worst case scenario? Boiled grubs. And I was so ravenous, it made no difference.

We dunked our bowls in the pot and found a clear place to squat...a place that was suddenly even clearer once Marok settled in. Something was going on. This was obviously not the best time to ask about it—though even if we were back in the privacy of his house, I doubted he would enlighten me.

Turned out, if there were grubs in the stew, they tasted suspiciously like venison.

Even though Marok helped himself to three bowls, he finished his food first, since he could swallow it while it was still scaldingly hot. He waited blandly while we finished. As Bess and I were slurping up every last dreg, he suddenly shot to his feet, startling me so badly I nearly tipped onto my ass. I stood just as quickly, though my knees protested and pins and needles played through my feet.

A pair of stout orcs approached. They were decorated with feathers and white paint—the shaman's men.

Don't stare.

I turned my gaze to the back of Marok's elbow and fixed the orcs in my peripheral vision.

"Taruut is ready now," one of them said. "You will surrender the humans."

They say that prisoners sometimes form an inexplicable bond with their captors. I'd never taken much stock in that. Until now. Maybe that phenomenon was at play...or maybe I just preferred the devil I knew.

Compared to what we'd suffered at the slaver's hands, Marok's treatment of us was downright genteel. But who knew what we could expect from the shaman?

"You've left them unchained?" one of the shaman's men asked.

Marok shrugged. "I hardly saw the point. They have tiny, blunt teeth and no claws whatsoever. No weapons, and nowhere to run. But if you're afraid of them...."

"Never mind," snapped the shaman's man, then gave me a shove to the shoulder that nearly flattened me. "This way—and I'm not in the mood to go chasing you. So don't get any dumb ideas."

He didn't need to tell me twice. Though as I headed off to wherever he was taking me, I did turn and glance over my shoulder to steal one last look at Marok. All I saw, however, was his broad back as he returned to his house without a parting glance.

15

QUINN

The shaman didn't live in a timber structure like the other orcs. His dwellings were in a hollowed-out cave system carved into the side of the bluff. It seemed like a naturally occurring space, but it was lavishly decorated with intricate carvings and strange symbols painted across the lintel. Some in chalky white, some in yellow ochre...and some clearly in the russet brown of dried blood. "Kneel for Taruut, you savage," the shaman's man barked, prodding me behind the knee with the butt of his spear.

I folded involuntarily to the ground, landing hard in the packed dirt, as Bess quickly knelt beside me. A curtain of small, painted bones strung together covered the broad opening—hundreds upon hundreds of bones—and they gave off a sifting clatter when the shaman came through. He was borne on his sedan chair by his team of four strong orcs, who placed him at the front of the opening, then stood with their hands resting on the hilts of the long knives at their hips.

At home, the shaman dispensed with the feathers and jewels in which he'd greeted us earlier, but his blind eyes were the same unsettling pale jade. He whiffed the air and said, "Well, if it isn't the humans."

The butt of a spear jabbed me in the kidney. "When the shaman speaks to you, you reply. *Taruut the Wise, we are unworthy.*"

That was gonna bruise. I repeated the phrase, keeping my eyes planted on the ground at the shaman's gnarly feet.

"Don't punish their ignorance," Taruut said. "I may have picked up plenty about humans and their ways on my Great Journey, but these two have yet to learn much about orcs. Now, if you see this one coming at me with a handy rock, feel free to cave in his skull." He chuckled…though I kind of doubted he was joking. "But humans are too fragile to withstand much discipline—so save it for deliberate infractions."

I risked a glance back at the orc with the spear…who was eyeing me like he was eager for me to pick up a rock and give him a reason to punish me.

"You will learn our ways soon enough," Taruut said. "What's left for me is to learn why you are here. Tossing the Ivories only told me of the one called Archibald. His purpose is clear…but yours is still shrouded in mystery. For now, the Slumbering Whale is just about ready to rouse. Let's get the stink of the slavers' tent off you."

The guard was only slightly less gentle when he shoved me with the spear butt and told me to get up and walk. If I ever had the chance, I'd be sure to return the favor—though

I was careful to avoid eye contact while I tried to memorize his face. Contrary to Marok's opinion of me, I'm not stupid.

We were hustled through the bone curtain and into a huge cavern. About half of the rock formations were natural, while half were carved into chunky, fantastical shapes of animals and faces. Nothing like the effete statuary of my last employer, which was delicate, gilded, and indistinguishable from the art in any other lavish estate. But what the orcish statuary lacked in finesse, it more than made up for in scale and abundance.

Not to mention horror.

Fortifications artwork was all about symmetry, prettiness, and polish. But the carved figures in the cavern walls looked like they could tear themselves free at any moment...and eat you alive.

The forbidding entrance chamber branched off into smaller tunnels and the floor sloped down, leading us deeper into the earth. "Orcs weren't made to live underground," Taruut told us. "We are green, like the moss and trees and grasses, not stony gray like the dwarves and their gnomish cousins. But when the Earth offers you Her treasures, you'd be a fool to turn them down.

"Hurry, now," Taruut instructed his porters. "The Whale is running early today—I can smell it. She'll spout soon." Over his shoulder, he said, "I've got the best nose in the village. With age comes infirmity...but also its own kind of power."

I hurried along after him before Spear-Butt could prod a fresh welt into my back.

The tunnel was long, lit only by the occasional oil-burning lantern. What sort of fat might be smoldering, I couldn't say. But it smelled worse than a flatulent ox.

"Sulfur," Taruut called back. "Farts of the earth." My skin prickled as I wondered if he'd just read my mind. Could he *smell* what I was thinking? Weirder things had happened. Hell, a week ago, I'd thought orcs themselves were nothing more than fairytales.

The smell thickened, as did the atmosphere, by the time the tunnel let out into a deep grotto. The large chamber was embellished, but not as aggressively as the entrance. The earth itself had done most of the sculpting here, twisting the living rock into strange and haunting forms. Stalactites dripped from the ceiling and the walls glistened with subtle striations of color. Despite the flickering of at least a dozen lanterns, the room was dark, and moist...and surprisingly warm.

In the center of the room was a bowl-shaped divot with a few inches of water on the bottom, maybe three times as wide as I was tall.

And to one side, on a pallet, was the limp body of Archie.

Immediately, images of him being sacrificed in some profane orcish ritual sprang to mind—rituals culminating with his blood painting the antechamber and his bones dangling from a doorway. But then he coughed, and shifted...and a young orc blotted his forehead with a damp cloth.

Taruut's carriers set down his litter in what looked to be a customary spot, before a table spread with food and drink, and a curious stick with a curved tip—which the Shaman immediately picked up and used to scratch vigorously at his back. "Ahh...much better. Now, if there's anything on you that can't get wet, set it off to the side. Then go stand in the Bowl of the Whale. Don't dally. She's almost nigh."

Neither Bess nor I had anything of value to speak of. I'd

lost my good boots and belt to the slavers, not to mention my whip, hunting knife, and whatever else would fetch them a few pennies. But I toed off my crude shoes and began to strip off my shirt.

"Leave it on," Taruut said—how did he *know*? "It stinks like a slave cage."

The guards herded Bess and me down into the stone depression and left us standing in the ankle-deep water. It was warm—again, surprisingly warm. And after two days' marching to leave the goblins behind, it actually felt good on my tired feet. I was flexing my toes gratefully when I noticed the first bubbles. Just a few, initially. But then, before I knew it, the surface of the water was roiling harder than the stew cauldron in the mess hall. A warning tremor danced across the soles of my feet, but my mind caught up with it a split second too late.

A blast of steaming, sulfurous water knocked me off my feet. It was so powerful it filled my nose, ears and mouth. Hell, I think even my ass got a thorough clean-out, right through my trousers. The water shot high, to the top of the cave—then hit the ceiling and rained down on us in huge, fat drops. By the time I realized I wasn't drowning and found my footing again, the blast fizzled to an abrupt stop, leaving nothing behind but a pair of spluttering wretches, the hollow sound made by a chorus of plinks and plunks....

And the rasp of thin laughter. "Oh, the looks on your faces," Archie wheezed.

"Save your breath, young one," Taruut told him. "I still sense the Plains of the Ancestors beckoning all around you."

"Huh—your ancestors, or mine?" Archie murmured as his eyelids fluttered closed.

Bess's clothes hung from her like sodden rags, and my clothes were no better. But, I had to admit, even with the lingering traces of sulfur, I smelled a heck of a lot better than I had since, weeks ago, I strode out through the Fortifications' walls. This "purification" I'd been vaguely dreading since I'd heard about it in the village square was nowhere near as sinister as I'd feared.

Taruut raised his head and inhaled deeply. "The Great Whale sure packs a wallop. Too bad I can't see your expressions—but you certainly do smell more reasonable. Now... let's get on with the purification."

My stomach sank.

The grotto of the geyser held many small offshoots. The guards prodded us into a chamber about the size of Marok's house, with waist-high stone shelves in the walls carved from the natural rock. A massive brazier lit the room, but also filled it with a haze of smoke and the smell of smoldering herbs. Taruut's litter was deposited before a ledge stuffed with boxes and bottles and bundles, and his bent fingers moved over his collection of herbs and trinkets, relearning their places.

"Off with the clothes," he said, and since Spear Butt was obviously eager for a reason to give me another bruise, I quickly complied, making sure to keep my eyes off Bess. If it was hard for me, it must be twice as bad for her. It was warm in the room—even stifling—and my clothes were drenched. Still, removing them made me feel vulnerable. Like I was putting all my tenderest parts on display—and giving a very delicate target to some bully with a spear.

It didn't help that the guard glanced down at my nakedness and smirked around his tusks.

"Now, then." Taruut hefted a pale, fist-sized stone in his hand. No...not a stone. A porcupine skull. "Get up on the bench and we'll see how much bad energy you've dragged into our village."

Whatever I thought "purification" would involve, it definitely wasn't this. Over the next several hours, Taruut piled us with various charms and sprinkled us with pungent herbal tinctures. He waved bundles of twigs in complicated gestures and drew patterns in the smoke from the brazier with a red-painted femur.

There were no words involved. He didn't pray, not like the sanctimonious clerics in the Fortifications prayed while they skimmed money from their congregations' tithings. But his motions were all guided by some internal impulse and carried out with great purpose.

Eventually, he sagged back in his sedan chair and said, "I have done all I can do. Stay here until I send for you, and clear your minds of the sour influence clinging to your spirits."

16

MAROK

My home felt empty. I stood in the common room and tried to figure out what was any different from before I set off to buy the slaves. Everything was in its place. I'd swept the barkberry from the floorboards. I'd even scrubbed out the hearth.

But none of that could erase the scent the humans had left behind.

In particular, Quinn's.

Not because his scent was any sharper than the female's, but because I associated it now with the feel of his nimble fingers tending my wound. Of his arms circling my waist as he tied on the dressing...and the way his arousal spiked when we pressed up against each other.

I had never coupled with a human before, though a few of my fellow soldiers had. Orc marriages are sacred, so it's not unusual to turn to some other race for a bit of variety. I'd mingled with a hobgoblin or two in my younger days. But once I married, I'd never felt the need.

Akala would often tease me with stories about the many ogre suitors of hers—suitors who never actually existed. She teased me about many things, from the sound of my snoring to the size of my feet.

But this was just her talk. Her actions proved her dedication was fierce—like the time she'd heard the wife of one of my soldiers muttering about me working them too hard, she'd put a stop to the complaining with a hearty swing of her favorite cudgel.

I opened a nearby chest and pulled out a cloth-wrapped bundle, trying to imagine the club in Akala's strong hands. Taruut had advised me to burn the thing on her pyre, but I simply couldn't do it. I ran my fingers along the scarred wood, then brought the weapon to my nose, searching yet again for traces of troll blood.

I found none. I never did. The beast who'd torn her apart had crept up on her so quietly, she hadn't gotten in even a single hit.

The familiar jingle of a traveling merchant's bell shook me out of the ugly memory, and I quickly wrapped the cudgel and stowed it away.

Only a few itinerant peddlers were willing to visit the Clan of the Red Hand since our periodic skirmishes with Two Swords turned into a war. The goblins were the first to stop coming, since they only have a taste for danger when they're the ones bringing the fight. The dwarves were glad for a reason to shut themselves up in their mountain and wait for us to get desperate enough to take our weapons repairs to them. Only the hobgoblins still made the trip....

Them, and the man standing there on the cobblestones outside my home grinning at me. The one who called himself Silver.

He looked like a sharp-featured human, though his scent told a different story—as did the small points on the tips of his ears. He claimed to be an elf. Though whether he thought anyone would truly fall for such a ridiculous tall tale, I'll never know.

Looking me square in the eye, he gave the bells on his cart a saucy jingle. "Ripe, juicy figs for sale, ten for a penny. Or maybe you're more of a nut-man." He jiggled a bag of walnuts. "All the way from the coast."

"These are gifts for receptive females," I snapped. "Why waste your breath hawking this sort of thing to me? There's no one here I need to impress."

"No? Big, strong brute like you—how is it one of the local ladies hasn't managed to snag your attention? I'd imagine you're quite the catch." Akala's death was common knowledge, but other than steadfast Borkul, Silver was the only one audacious enough to speak of it—even if it was only to hint at her being gone. "Or...maybe you're not *interested* in the ladies anymore. For the right price, we can have a good time, you and me...and I'll throw in the walnuts for free."

Silver wasn't exactly a whore—but he'd do just about anything for coin. Independence like his came at a price, and keeping himself well-provisioned wasn't cheap.

If he visited our stronghold more than twice a year, he'd know perfectly well that I was no longer the "catch" I might have once been. But that wouldn't matter to him, so long as I could pay.

Which I could afford to do. And he looked human enough that it would be so easy to pretend....

But even as I entertained the idea, the wind shifted, carrying his scent in my direction. Not only was it the odd whiff of unknown lineage...but the utter lack of arousal. This would be a business transaction for him, of course. Only a fool would think otherwise.

It only made me dwell on the memory of the sharp, musky desire I'd tasted when Quinn had slid his arms around me.

I hadn't been planning on buying anything from the peddler, but the thought of the human's scent changed my mind. With any luck, there was something in this mass of trinkets to obliterate it. "Show me your incense."

Silver's practiced smile grew slightly more genuine at the promise of a sale. "With pleasure."

17

QUINN

We'd been toasting by the open brazier in the grotto for quite a while when Archie rolled over on his slab and knuckled his eyes. "It's sweatier than a bricklayer's balls in here... but I guess it beats the slaver's tent."

"How are you feeling?" Bess asked him, but when she moved to get up, he motioned her to stay put. Taruut had placed various stones and trinkets on our bodies, and it seemed unwise to dislodge them.

"It hurts when I breathe," Archie admitted, uncharacteristically grim. "Hurts bad. I knew a guy once with a cough like this. First it was a nuisance, then it got serious...and the next thing you know he was in a charnel pit, snug under a blanket of quicklime. Taruut has made me his pet project—but I'm not sure all the shaman's bone-waving is doing me much good."

While Bess and I had been under Marok's taciturn watch, Archie had been privy to not only the shaman, but all his men. I couldn't speak for orcs, but all the soldiers I knew talked among themselves. "Have you heard anything while you were here—anything we can use to our advantage?"

"Just a bunch of badmouthing. Apparently, your pal Marok isn't exactly the darling of his clan."

"Kind of hard to miss," I said, thinking about the way none of them would even look at him.

"But he's got this huge house filled with all kinds of stuff," Bess said. "He must be rich, or important, or both. You'd think everyone would be bending over backward to get on his good side."

Maybe he didn't have a good side.

"Well," Archie said, dropping his voice dramatically—like someone who had to either vie for men's attentions, or go to bed with an empty belly. "From what I heard, he *used* to be some kind of big-shot. A real badass general. But a major battle of his went all to shit, and now he's being snubbed by the whole clan."

That was about all he'd gleaned, since he found himself sleeping more often than not. But even without the details, it explained a lot.

Eventually, Taruut returned in his litter and subjected Bess and me to a thorough scrutiny. By that, I mean sniffing. His proximity was disconcerting as he leaned over my naked body and inhaled. Up close, I could see the leathery texture of his skin, fissured with deep wrinkles. His tusks, nearly brown, had been etched with mystical symbols and filled in with gold. And then there were his eyes—just the shadow of a pupil still visible under the filmy greenish-white haze.

He grunted, and his exhalation played across my bare chest, raising gooseflesh on my arms that I didn't dare chafe away. "We are not merely beings of flesh and blood and bone," he said, "but a collection of our own thoughts and deeds. Orcs know their place in the world, and they lead very structured lives. But other races..." he made a vague gesture. "Their pasts tangle around them like torn fishing nets. And you.... I sense you have some conflict you tried to leave behind—but did not quite succeed."

Like any decent purveyor of mumbo-jumbo, the shaman was great at making grandiose statements that someone might take to heart—but when you looked at them closely enough, they could very well apply to anyone. Luckily, he wasn't seeking my agreement. In an orc's eyes, a human (or any other non-orc) was only one step above an animal, and our opinions didn't exactly count.

Taruut took another good whiff of me. "And yet, you're more than just a vessel to be rinsed clean in the river. The traces of your past are responsible for who you are today. There is still strife in your future, I think. Whether it will break you or make you stronger remains to be seen."

A guard with streaks of white clay on his cheeks strode through the door and presented himself to Taruut, kneeling. "Borkul is here to bring them to the chieftain."

Taruut waved him to his feet. "Fine. I've done all I can for these two. The rest is out of my hands."

Borkul came in and produced the expected genuflection, then dumped a bundle of cloth on the cavern floor. "It's been a few seasons since my kids were small enough to fit in these old things. Lucky my wife hadn't traded them off to the peddler."

Taruut sniffed in their direction. "I'm sure they're preferable to wandering around naked." Wait...they got rid of our *clothes*? "There's a nip in the air. And human constitutions are notoriously fragile. Bundle up the horseman and the girl and be on your way."

"What about the boy?" Borkul asked.

Taruut smiled cryptically to himself. "Archibald's place is with me...for now."

Was it weird to be happy to see Borkul? Maybe *happy* was a strong word. More like relieved—because although he was the whole reason goblins attacked our camp to begin with, at least he'd never punched a massive bruise into my back with the butt of a spear.

Guess my standards were getting pretty low.

Back when I first set off from the Fortifications, I'd brought along a few solid, well-made items of clothing. Those were obviously long gone, stripped off by the marauders who'd knocked me out and dragged me to the dreaded tent. I'd been marched to the orc camp in slavers' rags.

The clothing Borkul had brought was strange—woven fabrics reinforced with patches of suede at the elbows and knees, boxy fitting, without buttons or ties. Definitely better than the rags from the slavers, but when I pulled the tunic over my head, the smell hit me. Not filth. Not sweat. Earthen and strong, but nothing I could quite put my finger on, either—other than to say it reminded me of Marok's house.

So it could only have been...the smell of orc.

If I felt out of place in my oversized pajama-like outfit, Bess was even more ridiculous, drowning in a tunic made for someone twice her size. I wondered what had become of her handkerchief...and decided it wasn't worth another bruise to find out.

"We didn't have an extra pair of boots lying around," Borkul said, "and even if we did, they'd never fit your weird feet." For the record, plenty of men found my feet very attractive. "Lucky for you there's a peddler in town, and I've still got a few coins left over from the slaver's. But let's get moving before his cart is picked clean."

It was a relief to walk out of the shaman's caves under Borkul's command, even if that did mean being tethered to Bess with a leather leash like a team of skittish colts. This time, when we walked through the settlement, people not only stared, but also tried to waylay us by striking up a conversation.

I'd thought orcs were just dour and hidebound people. But Borkul's evident popularity had me seeing Marok in a whole new light. "Can I ask you something?" I ventured when Bess and I were alone with him.

"You just did." He smirked around his tusks at his own joke, then said, "Go ahead—as long as you understand that inside the chieftain's lodge, the guard won't be so tolerant."

"It's just...everyone acts so funny toward Marok. Everyone but you."

"I'm his heart-brother," he said simply.

I glanced at Bess to see if she got what that was supposed to mean, and she shrugged.

"I don't know the term," I finally admitted, wondering if that meant they were cousins, or brothers-in-arms, or what. "You're related...how?"

"By marriage." His easy voice grew strained. "He was husband to my sister."

Was?

Oh.

That might explain a few things. Marok's shut-down atti-tude. The big, empty house. The certain things we weren't allowed to touch. "Did he lose her before or after the failed campaign?"

"Before. Once Akala was gone, he threw himself into battle. But grief makes us blind." Something dark flickered across his face, then disappeared.

Of course, I had more questions.

But while Borkul might be pretty easygoing compared to his clanmates, I wasn't about to test his patience by pursuing something he clearly didn't want to discuss.

The peddler had set up his cart in the orc village square, and he'd attracted a small mob of shoppers. Mostly orcs, but a few races I didn't recognize, either, each different from the other—and each with a strange symbol branded on their cheek, like the poor creature tending the latrines. A mark.

A slave mark.

If that was my fate...so much for my throngs of eager ad-mirers back in the Fortifications. Not that I'd be likely to ever cross their paths again anyhow.

"Clear out," Borkul called to the crowd. "We're here on Ul-Rott's business." With a few grumbles, the orcs wrapped up their haggling and dispersed. Borkul flipped me a few coppers, then did the same for Bess, who snatched them neatly out of the air. "Get what you need. But be quick about it. Don't wanna keep the chieftain waiting."

The last few orcs cleared out, and I finally got a look at the peddler. I must've been expecting an orc. Or a goblin. Or one of those pig-faced monstrosities I'd seen in the bazaar.

I was not prepared for the man I did see—whose interest

perked up the moment he laid eyes on me.

Decked out from head to toe in decayed finery, he was no more an orc than I was...though when I spied his pointed ears, I saw he was no human, either. A coat of tattered brocade. Longish chestnut hair tied back with a satin ribbon. Skin-tight breeches of fine doeskin worn smooth at the seams. Scuffed thigh-high boots tied below the knee with the fraying remains of colorful scarves. And cheekbones to make anyone stop and look twice.

The peddler locked eyes with me and smiled a slow, cryptic grin. "Well, well, well. What have we here?"

"We need shoes," Bess said. "And whatever else you can think of that we won't be able to find in this village."

Though it was Bess who'd spoken, the peddler held my gaze for a heartbeat before turning his attention to her. He might be foreign to me, but I knew the look. It was the look of a man who'd meet you back behind the tavern...with his trousers down.

"I'm no cobbler," the man said, "but let's see if I can't dig up something from my treasure trove." That said with a lascivious glance at me. "Name's Silver, by the way. Costermonger extraordinaire. If I don't have what you need now, I can make it a point to swing back with it in a fortnight." He sauntered up to me and lowered his voice. "But I suspect I may indeed have *exactly* what you're looking for."

Orcs have good hearing, but Borkul had dropped our leash and was busy chatting with a couple of orcish soldiers on the far side of the square. As Bess rifled through the cart in search of useful items, I eased closer to Silver and pitched my voice low. "What is it you think I'm looking for?"

His smile deepened. "A way out...of course." He indicated

his cart with a flick of his eyes. It was deep enough to hold someone if they curled up just so, pulled by a single docile mule. "But I'd only have room to smuggle out one."

This was it. My chance to get away from the Clan of the Red Hand before someone branded my face, or cut off my arm...or worse. Of course, I was tempted. But then I watched Bess trying to force her feet into a pair of too-small slippers and said, "If you take anyone, it should be her."

"She wasn't the one I invited, though, was she?" After treating me to a lingering head-to-toe look, he added, "I'm not just keen on someone to share my bedroll. It's tough out there—tougher than you think. I'd need someone who could swing a sword...although it wouldn't hurt if he looked as fetching as you while doing it."

Silver wasn't my usual type—too lean and pretty by half— but it would hardly be a chore to pass some time with him. Intellectually, I knew I'd be an idiot to refuse the offer. But somehow, I didn't feel quite right about sneaking out. "There's no way you'd get past the gate without them smelling me a mile off. And once they do," I flapped the leather leash for emphasis, "it's back in the neck irons for me."

"They've got quite the sense of smell, to be sure, but there are ways of putting my scent on you. And yet, since you haven't jumped at the chance to be my...traveling companion..." he smiled his cryptic smile. "I'll not waste my breath trying to convince you. Clearly, you've got a very good reason to stay."

"I just know better than to invite more trouble than I already have."

"Oh, but the best trouble always comes uninvited." Now he was only bantering with me for form's sake. He cut his eyes to Borkul in the distance. "I doubt you're as boring as you make yourself out to be. Maybe you've just taken a particular fancy to the color green."

I scoffed, which only seemed to convince him otherwise.

"No? Correct me if I'm wrong, but your accent tells me you've spent your life inside the Fortifications' walls. Why *wouldn't* you find yourself intrigued by an orc? After all that stultifying Fortifications nonsense about where you can or can't put your dick, it's positively liberating to be around creatures with such relaxed customs about who can share their furs."

"How so?" I asked carefully.

"Haven't any of them approached you yet?"

I gave my leash another pointed shake. "Not much opportunity for mingling."

Silver bent over his cart, casually presenting his rump for my inspection, then straightened up with a pair of boots in his hand—human-sized boots. He tossed them to the ground at my feet, then said, "Orcs pair off, man and woman, faithful as can be...among themselves. But as far as the rest of us two-legged animals are concerned, anything goes. Y'see, in their eyes, the rest of us aren't exactly people. Close enough to tryst with...but not in the same category as their own kind. They don't even consider it a breach of vows. An orc would no sooner pitch a fit about a human dalliance than get jealous of their lover's left hand."

So that thing I picked up on with the goblins outside the bazaar was normal...for an orc.

Silver kept talking while I pulled on the boots—his spare pair, he claimed, which he was deigning to sell me only as a personal favor. Hardly as good a fit as the custom pair I'd lost to the slavers—not to mention the ridiculous decorative tooling around the cuffs—but they'd do.

"If an orc decided to add you to his or her menagerie, no one would so much as blink—not even their dear spouse! Well, they might grumble a little..." he smirked. "Though the orcs wealthy enough to expand their households are few and far between, since most of the younger ones live in those communal barracks over by the well. But the older, more established orcs—the tradesmen, the artisans, the high-ranking warriors? Not unusual for those with the extra space to keep a slave around the house. Not unusual at all."

Marok had the whole house to himself. And since he was a widower...no one to grumble.

Which was clearly none of my business whatsoever.

When we'd outfitted ourselves the best we could, I found a ha'penny leftover...and spied a delicate slip of fine cloth pinned to his display. "And I'll take that handkerchief. For the lady."

Silver arched an eyebrow...but handed it over without a word.

18

QUINN

If Marok's house was surprisingly large, the chieftain's lodge was palatial. Appearances, I was beginning to learn, meant everything around here. And Ul-Rott the Spinecrusher would hardly strike terror into the hearts of his enemies living in a simple hut.

To say I wasn't given the grand tour would be putting it mildly. Borkul marched me around to the stables and handed me off to the guy in charge, a grizzled old orc with half an ear missing. "Be a good little human," Borkul said, "and maybe you'll earn the chieftain's brand. Or be a slacker and get a beating. It's all up to you."

Bess shot me a forlorn look over her shoulder as he led her inside the building. And then it was just me, the half-eared orc...and the biggest damn horse I'd ever laid eyes on. It was a thick, muscular creature the color of autumn hay, at least three hands taller than my largest stallion, with a wild, tangled black mane and hooves as big around as dinner plates.

"This here's Destroyer," said the half-eared orc, shoving me into the pen. "Go ahead and show us what you got."

Horses aren't predators—they're prey. But that doesn't make them any less dangerous. This great beast could crush a man with a single blow of his massive hoof, I had no doubt. And the way he reared up when I intruded on his space was a clear warning to keep my distance.

Some trainers will beat a horse into submission, but that's never been my style. What I want from a horse isn't broken surrender, but partnership. The way you hold yourself is critical. Horses read body language. And while I have two legs, not four, I could still communicate with my stance. To present myself as not a threat—but a leader.

"Go on," called Half-ear. "Do something."

I was doing something. I was demonstrating to Destroyer that I wouldn't harm him...but that I wasn't afraid of him, either. The leather leash dangling from my neck served as a makeshift whip—too short and far less flexible than the braided whip I'd lost in the Wastelands. But I never used it to punish an animal. Only to snag his attention and put it where I needed it.

Judging by the scars on Destroyer's hide, he'd seen his share of the whip already.

I stood in the center of the round enclosure, stance easy, while the horse shifted away from me. Never get behind a horse—especially one as powerful as this. A single kick could be enough to end your career. Or even your life.

And so it began, the part of the process I think of as "the dance." Destroyer circling the pen. Me in the center, confident and calm, watching for signals. You can always tell what a horse thinks of you if you know what to look for. It's in the cant of the ears. The tension of the neck. And always...the eyes.

Horses aren't generally aggressive. Sure, they might challenge one another for a better position in the herd...but *fear* is what makes them attack. Destroyer flicked his ears forward, a good sign, and began to regard me with curiosity. It was a critical first step in building a partnership.

Keeping myself right in the center of the enclosure, I tapped my whip against my thigh when his focus started to wander, and soon had him trotting circles around the pen, with me at the hub of the action. Destroyer was smart and confident, and with the proper handling, he'd make an awesome steed.

It would take a few more sessions until he let me get close enough to touch him—let alone bridle and saddle him—but this initial encounter was a great start. He was starting to trust me. To understand where I wanted him to go by watching my body language. To give me his attention when I cracked the whip for attention. To *respond*. I turned toward the stable to let him have a well-earned rest. Only then did I realize my audience was no longer just Half-ear.

The orc who'd joined him probably wasn't much bigger than the other orcs (who, frankly, were all massive) but he was way more scary. It wasn't the crown of twisted bones, and it wasn't the broadsword strapped to his back that likely weighed more than me. It was his eyes. Clever enough to take in everything, but with a flinty hardness utterly devoid of mercy.

Like the alpha in a pack of wild horses, some individuals

have an aura of leadership—and Ul-Rott the Spinecrusher was one of them. I've never thought much of authority,
finding most people in charge ended up there by dumb
luck. So the urge to kneel took me by surprise. Lucky for
me, Destroyer was familiar enough with me that he didn't
take the opportunity to trample me flat.

"So, you're some kind of expert," Ul-Rott said, like he'd
only believe it when he saw it.

"Yes, sir."

The half-eared orc snorted.

Ul-Rott said, "Your people's 'sir' means nothing here. Hon-
or me with my name."

I bit back a reflexive *yes, sir.* "Yes, Ul-Rott."

"Stand," he said, and I straightened up. "At least you've
survived so far in the same pen as Destroyer. That's more
than I expected from such a soft little thing. But no bridle?
No saddle?"

"He needs more time, Ul-Rott. If you take things too
fast—"

"Step aside, human," snapped the half-eared orc. "I got
the bridle on him once and I'll do it again."

Ignoring my plea to wait, he shoved into the corral,
scooped up the bridle, and charged at the horse. It was the
perfect storm: orc, bridle and horse, everything converg-
ing at once. Destroyer reared up, eyes wide, and punched
out with a dinner-plate hoof. There was a sickening crunch
of bone—and Destroyer wound up again to finish what he
started.

"Down!" I barked, snapping the whip hard against my
thigh. My gut wanted me to run away, to get somewhere safe
while that orc got exactly what he deserved. But my mind

knew there was no safety for me here. Not unless I proved my worth. And so I squared my shoulders, projected all the confidence I could muster, and hoped to hell that the fragile, new bond I'd forged with the horse would still hold.

He reared again...then backed away, leaving the half-eared orc moaning in the dirt.

Destroyer wasn't thrilled about the situation—the whites of his eyes were still showing. But he'd obeyed.

Fuming over the amount of progress that dumbass had just cost us, I clucked my tongue and herded the horse toward the stable without waiting for permission. Thankfully, no one stopped me, and the act of feeding and watering him gave me the time I needed to calm down so I wouldn't say anything stupid. I was right. Of course I was. But like I'd learned at the slavers' tent, being right didn't make a damn bit of difference when someone else held all the power.

A couple of burly orcs were loading Half-ear onto a litter. A jagged spike of bone protruded from his upper arm. He bellowed when they moved him, and a spray of dark, rust-colored blood fountained from the wound.

Ul-Rott looked on with no more emotion than I would've shown watching a sparrow fly away, then turned to me said, "How long until you bridle him?"

"A week."

"We're at war with the Two Swords Clan. You have three days."

Any relief I might have felt over winning the chieftain's tacit approval drained away when I saw my new quarters. The loft above the stable was hardly a loft at all. More like a few brittle planks thrown across the beams. There was nothing stored up there but a few coils of rope and some empty feed sacks. In all likelihood, it wouldn't even support the weight of a full-grown orc. Bats hung from the peak of the roof and the smell of animal was thick. And when I curled up that night on my scratchy feed-sack bed—cold and exhausted, with horseflies buzzing in my ears—I wondered what the hell I'd been thinking when I turned down Silver's offer of escape.

19

MAROK

Normally, my day would begin with a hobgoblin runner bringing orders from Ul-Rott. I might put my warriors through some training. Or I might join the chieftain for a strategic planning session. I might even be invited to dine at his table.

But since the last battle—the one where Two Swords decimated my troop—runners no longer came.

I'd hoped Ul-Rott would be pleased with the humans we'd found. The shaman only expected the boy, after all, and we'd come back with two more, both of them with skills that would make our clan stronger. But if Ul-Rott was impressed with my find, I'd heard no tell of it.

Three days. It had been three days since we made our way back through the southern hunting grounds, and still, no runner. I'd arranged and re-arranged my collections, swept the plank floor until it started to splinter, and even aired out my pelts...though despite a good airing, I could still smell human on them.

I could still smell Quinn.

It was late in the morning, far too late for a runner, and I was through telling myself that maybe they were just late, maybe they were on a new rotation, maybe they were just around the corner, if only I gave them a few more minutes. I finally admitted to myself that there would be no runner. I had no orders.

I had no purpose.

As punishments went, I used to think that shunning was far too lax. What hardship would there be, I wondered, in simply being ignored?

And now...I understood.

If I were exiled, left to wander the woods, I'd find my purpose soon enough. Shelter, food, protection from enemies. All these things would keep me so busy, I'd have little time to reflect on my own failings. But within the shelter of the Red Hand's walls—within the home I'd once shared with Akala—thinking was the only thing I *could* do.

Fine. If I couldn't help my clan ready itself for the next battle, I could at least feed us. When I geared up for a hunt and headed out into the woods, no one challenged me. For that matter, no one even spoke to me. Even as they opened the gate, the guards—who had once competed to be in my troop—looked right through me as if I wasn't even there.

I tightened my grip on my spear and trod straight ahead.

I had hoped the forest might take my mind off my troubles, but instead it only reminded me how alone I was. It wasn't my impromptu hunting trips with Akala I was ruminating on, either. It was trekking through these very woods with Quinn.

Maybe Borkul was right. I should have just coupled with the horseman and got it out of my system. It's not like Ul-Rott would have smelled me on the human. As far as the chieftain was concerned, I no longer existed.

I trudged through the woods for hours, passing up the smaller prey so their blood scent didn't drive off the larger game. But eventually, I wondered if it even mattered. Whether I brought back a rabbit or a doe, the reaction would be the same. None at all. Could they afford to leave the carcass to rot, simply because the hunt was mine? Maybe I didn't want to find out.

I wasn't far from the clan, though I'd picked a route that was poorly traveled, owing to some awkward footing and the occasional stretch of quicksand. Maybe it would be easiest to find such a spot and let it suck me under. When the muck filled my lungs, the pain would be brutal—as it should be.

Seems there's never any quicksand around when you need it.

Soon, the rushing of Lame Stag River sounded in the distance and the scent of water was on the air. The scent of water...and orc.

I went still, placing my steps carefully so as not to rustle a leaf or snap a twig, and eased my way toward the riverbank. The Lame Stag's course was much the same here as it had been before the droughts that shuffled our territory with that of the Two Swords Clan. This land was swampy and rough. Had it even been fought over at all, the skirmishes would have been cursory, at best.

As I eased closer to the river, the scent of orc intensified.

I parted the trees and found a dozen orcs on the opposite bank—Two Swords orcs—and they were hard at work fording the deep river. From the looks of it, they'd been laboring for days. A good ton of rock had been shifted, and nearby wagon ruts ran deep. They weren't just creating a crossing for a hunting party, either. They were paving the way for an army.

How long would it take them to finish their task—a week? Not even. Maybe as little as a few days.

I'd come hunting in a search for purpose...and I'd found it. My senses sharpened, and I was aware of everything, from the midges swarming around my eyes seeking their salty moisture, to my position and bearing and the direction of the wind. I eased away with excruciating care, so taut my muscles sang with tension, until finally I deemed myself well out of earshot. I let out a shaking breath, then gathered my strength...and ran.

The gate guards were so alarmed at the sight of me barreling up the path that they forgot to act indifferent. They swung the doors wide without challenge, and watched, wide-eyed, as I rushed up the road to Ul-Rott's lodge. The guards at the chieftain's gate were all veterans, older than the gate guards, and not so easily impressed. A pair of formidable warriors stood in my path, and they showed no signs of moving.

"I will speak to Ul-Rott," I said, and they ignored it. "I will see him now."

The tone had always worked with my troops—but not now. Not anymore.

I would not beg. Yes, I had failed the clan. But I was *not* weak.

Through the doorway, a flash of armor caught my eye.

Very distinctive armor with straps of green tooled leather. I knew its owner well. "Raboth!" I called out. "We must speak. Now."

Raboth and I had trained together, and given each other our fair share of bumps and bruises along the way. Not only were we well-acquainted, but he held some authority. Enough to be able to think for himself.

"Two Swords is planning an attack," I told him as he strode out with a curious look on his face.

He spared me an appraising glance. "Oh?"

"They will cross the Lame Stag and attack from the south. We only have days, maybe just hours, to prepare. Our south flank is our weakest. We must get word to Ul-Rott and deploy the soldiers."

Raboth didn't answer. Simply stared.

"Take credit for it if you must," I said. "But Ul-Rott needs to know."

Raboth barked out a laugh. "As if anyone would take credit for your strategy after Two Swords fed your warriors to the crows!"

"But I saw—"

"You're lucky I don't have you beaten for disrupting my soldiers."

He wouldn't dare. The urge to challenge him to settle his insult with a fight was strong, but I tamped it down for the sake of the clan. "If you don't tell Ul-Rott, then I will. Stand aside."

"Now, now. You and I both know that if you barge into the lodge, the chieftain's personal guard will cave in your skull before you get within shouting distance. Tell you what. You declare that I'm the better swordsman, and I get you in without a fight."

Raboth might have the fancier armor—but my skills were sharper. His swings were wild and his form was lacking. But pride had its place. And my pride would do me no good if my whole clan suffered the same fate my troop had at the hands of the Two Swords Clan. "You are the better swordsman. Your arm is strong and your blade is keen. And your troops are proud to call you leader."

Raboth stared at me for a heartbeat, then threw back his head and guffawed. "The mighty Marok has learned humility? What's this world coming to?" Chortling to himself, he gestured for me to follow him. "Come, then, never let it be said that I don't keep my word."

He led me around the perimeter. Normally, I went straight through to the grand hall. But I was no longer privy to the day-to-day workings of the lodge, and figured he had his reasons. Though I sensed something was not right when instead of taking me inside, Raboth led me to the stables.

A flick of Raboth's hand had the guards parting to let us pass, but there was no Ul-Rott in the exercise yard. There was no one but a scattering of guards, a few grazing mules, and the backside of the stables.

"Today's the day your folly bears its bitter fruit," Raboth said gleefully.

"What do you mean?" I demanded.

"The horseman has done nothing since he got here—nothing but stand there in the pen while Destroyer trots circles around him. It's only fitting that you should be present to see this pet human of yours fail. If he doesn't bridle the useless horse by sundown, he'd better hope for a fast death. Though given who brought him here, I doubt Ul-Rott will be inclined to show him that mercy."

Dread settled, cold, in my gut. But if I didn't warn the chieftain the Two Swords Clan was coming, Quinn would likely die either way—along with most of my clan. "Forget the human. Take me to Ul-Rott."

"I never claimed I would take you to Ul-Rott. Just that I'd get you inside the lodge." He looked me square in the eye with a nasty smile. "Maybe while you're here, you should make yourself useful and muck out the stalls."

Rage boiled inside me, licking my guts, urging me to bury my fist in his laughing, smug face. It would feel so good. The crunch of bone. The snap of a broken tusk. No, not just good—right.

But spill his blood now, and I'd never stand before Ul-Rott.

Raboth strode off, still laughing to himself, leaving me behind in the exercise yard. Not because he trusted me, but because there was precious little here I could see or do. There weren't even many guards, just a pair at the gate and two more by the entrance to the main building. Why waste swords guarding a handful of mules and a warhorse no one could even touch?

I was about to turn on my heel and leave in disgust when the wind shifted—carrying with it the distinct smell of human.

No, not of any random human.

Of Quinn.

The sharpness of his sweat, the depth of his musk, all of it mingled now with the barnyard smell of grazing pack animals—but it was devoid of that hint of arousal I'd first scented on him out in the woods.

He was better off without me. The sooner he could make

his own mark in the lodge so the clan could forget about who'd found him, the stronger his position.

But I couldn't resist a quick parting look.

Sticking close to the stables, I made my way around the building and stood in the shadow of the roof's overhang. Destroyer was trotting in a circle. The horse's ears pricked as he spotted me, but Quinn didn't notice. He stood at the trough in just breeches and boots, coated in dust, with sweat painting dark rivulets down his chest and ribs. No wonder his scent carried so far. He was covered in sweat, and the tangy salt smell set my mouth to watering. It was strikingly different from an orcish scent. But the orcs I knew wanted nothing to do with me, which only made this difference even more enticing.

Despite the dust and dirt, the hard chisel of his muscle was clear. Though Quinn's human skin might be oddly smooth... he looked anything but soft.

As I watched, he grabbed a bucket from beside the trough and dipped it in, capturing some water. He upended the bucket right over his head, sluicing off the dirt and grit. And as he did, his scent blossomed, thick and heady. It filled the air with his utter humanness, welling around me, wreaking havoc with my common sense. I could practically taste the salt, feel the tang of him dance upon my tongue.

My breath quickened and my muscles tensed. Quinn threw his head back and shook out his long, dark hair. Droplets lit on his skin and hair like jewels, as runoff pooled beneath his boots. His scent should have been diluted. But it wasn't. It was purified.

Want blinded my actions. I knew that he was in a pen with a horse capable of snapping my spine with a single, well-placed kick, but I barged ahead anyway, unable to quell my relentless, urgent need. I shoved past the pen gates, seeing nothing but water-slicked human flesh, smelling nothing but Quinn's intoxicating human scent.

The sound of the gate startled him and he whirled around, spraying water. But though his heartbeat quickened, I smelled no fear on him. And as I crossed the pen, his expression shifted from surprise to curiosity. "Marok? Is everything okay—?"

I picked up speed as I strode toward him, and backed him up against the stable wall. His scent shifted. Not with fear—but with lust.

The regular beat of the horse's hooves, soft thumps on the dirt of the pen, skittered to a stop. Quinn shoved me back with the flat of his palm and commanded the horse, "Roy, down!"

The warhorse pranced in place...but obeyed.

Quinn scavenged a crabapple from his pocket and tossed it to the horse, who snatched it up and gobbled it down immediately. Quinn then cocked his head toward the barn. "We might want to head inside—just in case Roy changes his mind about you. He packs one hell of a kick."

"You gave the steed a human name."

"Destroyer was way too much of a mouthful. Besides, I think he prefers it."

I followed Quinn into the barn. Though light slanted in through the beams, it was dim and quiet inside, and the powerful smell of animal nearly blotted out the scent of Quinn—which only drew me closer, seeking more of that elusive, intoxicating human smell.

As I moved toward Quinn, he backed away, matching me

step for step. Not trying to evade me, though, simply keeping me in his sights. The distance he put between us, in fact, was small enough for me to reach out and throttle him—or grab him and drag him closer.

"Don't you fear me?" I asked.

"I can tell when something's a threat—it's what separates the average trainers from the great ones."

"That would make a difference...if I were an animal."

Quinn tossed his damp hair from his eyes and closed the gap between us with a decisive step. He pressed against me, stretched up on his toes, and whispered in my ear, "We're *all* animals."

That whisper exposed Quinn's tender neck—did he know what that did to me? I'm told only orcs give the baring of the throat such meaning—show your neck to a goblin and they'll tear out your jugular. But humans had no fangs, no tusks, so it might not mean the same. Even so, I dropped my face to the crook of his neck as I would with a lover, and I buried myself in his heady scent.

Which immediately turned musky and rich.

"You have some velvety fine whiskers I can't really see," he gasped. "And they feel...uh.... Wow." With a shaky breath, he squeezed a hand between us to reach down and adjust himself. His nimble human fingers then slid between the chinks in my armor, then paused over the wound I'd taken the night we met. "Is this okay?"

I grunted against his neck. "It heals."

"It's just...I feel responsible...."

"The knife was in the goblin's hand. Not yours." Besides, I could hardly feel the wound right now over the throbbing ache in my cock. I skimmed my tusks over his tender neck.

His impossibly smooth skin played across my lower lip, delicate and salty. So vulnerable.

And, apparently, so sensitive.

As my chin bristles scraped over his tender flesh, his breath caught and his arousal scent spiked—just as a telling hardness prodded me in the thigh. "Why does this please you?" I couldn't help but ask.

"Can't you tell?" Quinn said on a breathy laugh. "You're my type."

I stopped nuzzling him, confused. "An orc?"

"A man." He sank his fingers into my hair and encouraged me to go on. "I always went for the big ones. But they tend to act like they're doing you a favor. Lucky to get a tug on my dick in return for my troubles, let alone..." one hand ranged along my shoulders while the other cupped my cheek in a gentle caress. "This."

I pressed a knee between his legs and hitched him up higher so I could really bury my face in his scent, to breathe him all in, to lose myself in his arousal. As he rode my thigh, a broken sound escaped him. My haze of lust faltered, worried I'd shoved too hard and hurt him. But a grind of his hips—accompanied by a spike of the earthy scent of want—urged me to keep going.

"Damn, Marok—I'm gonna nut on you like a fourteen-year-old kid rubbing himself off at the bathhouse."

"Do it," I rumbled as I licked his collarbone to see if he tasted as good as he smelled.

Delicate salt blossomed over my tongue.

More than just good. Delicious.

"Yes—that—oh fuck."

While my ragged breaths fanned his throat, Quinn rutted

hard against my thigh. The sounds of pleasure wrenched from him drove me wild, made my blood surge hot. His muscles went taut, and he stilled, gasping...and then the tell-tale earthen scent of his spend enveloped my senses.

For just a moment, I was lost to the scent of the human.

For just a moment I was happy.

For just a moment, I'd forgotten who I was. And what I'd lost. And why I was even here.

But even a moment was more of a reprieve than I deserved.

Quinn slid off my thigh, raking his hair from his forehead, and reached for the lacings on my breeches. I shoved his hands away. "No—you don't want my scent on you."

"I may beg to differ."

"Listen to me." I pushed him back against the wall. A pink flush of satiation warmed his cheeks. He regarded me with heavy-lidded eyes and not a trace of fear. "I'm here to warn Ul-Rott there's an attack coming from the south, and my words are falling on deaf ears."

"Well...does the news have to come from you?"

"Do you think you could deliver it better?"

"Me? Hah. They'd be more likely to listen to the mules. But Borkul always seems to have your back. I mean, he's a goof, and pretty much the last guy I'd put on watch, but the stigma that's following you around doesn't extend to him."

Before I could second-guess myself, I grasped Quinn's face in both my hands and pressed my forehead to his. Head to head—heart to heart. Did humans do this? No idea. But what use was it to deny how I felt?

"I will tell my heart-brother—and save the clan."

20

QUINN

Marok was my type.

Marok.

An orc.

No one should be blamed for the random things they think in a fit of passion...but in that instant when I was riding his powerful thigh and reveling in the scrape of his whiskers against my skin, I knew. It wasn't just the heat of the moment.

It was true.

Not just because he was huge and well-muscled, rock hard and solid, everywhere. And not just because he'd taken a filthy stab-wound shielding me from a goblin attack. But because of the way he'd huffed into my neck while he got me off—like he could eat me right up.

It's heady to want someone...and better yet to be wanted in return.

I cleaned myself up and went back out to the pen, where

Roy was shoving his muzzle through the pickets of the fence, straining to nibble on a weed that was just out of reach. I clicked my tongue, and he turned and whickered a greeting. He was an intelligent horse—he caught on fast, and he already knew when to give me his attention, come to me, and (most importantly) stop. But he still shied away when I tried to touch him.

Any horse that smart should've been bridled by now. But if Roy was to be a good warhorse, I wanted more than just compliance. So I was leaving the bridle for the last possible moment to give our partnership as much time to develop as I dared.

Okay...who was I kidding? He was ridiculously big. Any horse can do serious damage with a blow of his hooves. But I'd seen Roy practically snap an orc in half, and that guy was a heck of a lot sturdier than me. I'm always taking a risk when I get into a pen with an untamed animal. Usually, that just makes me wary. But in Roy's case, I was scared.

I dropped the bit in the center of the pen and let Roy inspect it. Show no fear, I told myself. Easier said than done in this case. He was lipping the bridle on the ground when I sensed eyes on me, and turned, ready to defend my actions. But it wasn't Ul-Rott come to check up on me, or even one of his guards.

It was Bess.

If I didn't know she was the only human woman in the village, I wouldn't have recognized her. Gone were the slaver's rags, and gone was the ill-fitting linen outfit. Bess wore a pair of doeskin trousers laced up the sides, and a soft woolen shift cinched tight by an elaborately woven leather belt. Her sloppily shorn hair had been trimmed and all the grime washed out. Now it curled a bit—and its formerly mud-brown color was now the shade of golden wheat.

But the most striking difference of all was the angry, red brand on her cheek.

"Are you okay?" I gasped.

She seemed puzzled by the question. "Fine." She considered her own statement, then nodded decisively. "No, I'm pretty good."

"But your face—"

Her fingertips grazed the blistered mark. It was about as big as my thumb, three crossed spears with stars in between. "It didn't hurt. Not all that much. And now everyone knows which household I'm part of. The head blacksmith has me fixing their broken chainmail—apparently these orcs can't see anything up close, not like we can. He's bragging to anyone who'll listen that it's like having his very own dwarf—except I won't drink him out of house and home. He's feeding me well. And...he's got children. Daughters." She ran her fingers over the belt. "Youngest one's barely ten and I fit in all her clothes—she gets a real kick out of it. And one thing's for sure—they're a lot more respectful than the spoiled kids I minded in the Fortifications."

"Have you seen Borkul?" I asked, worried he'd fail to grasp the seriousness of the situation, even with Marok's warning.

"Not since we got here."

"He has an important message to deliver, so if you do see him—"

"Light a fire under his lazy butt. Got it."

Bess couldn't stay—she was expected at the smithy. But the fact that they let her walk around alone—after only a few days—was nothing short of baffling. Even if she ran, I supposed, she wouldn't get far. But maybe she didn't want to run.

After all, what could she expect back in The Fortifications but another lecherous employer with another vindictive wife? Or, worse, another stint in the slaver's tent?

Funny, I realized, as I watched her walk resolutely away. Even after Archie terrorized us with notions of being plowed by a massive orcish dong, Bess was thriving.

And I wouldn't have minded working my hand down Marok's pants and seeing what the equipment was really all about.

Roy was straining for that weed again, so I called him inside and forked out some fresh hay. He did listen—which was good. And I didn't need to worry about him caving in my skull while he scarfed down the hay, which was even better, since I could head up to my loft for a well-deserved nap. I'd hardly call it cozy now, even with the discarded horse blanket I'd scavenged forming a thin mattress. But it was better than the slaver's tent.

The stables were not what you'd call restful. Not only did the animals rustle around, but the orcs in the lodge were active day or night. As far as I could tell, their sleep had no natural rhythm—maybe because they relied on their noses instead of their eyes to take stock of their surroundings. Which meant I had to steal my shut-eye when I could, because I never knew when an orc would show up demanding a progress report.

The fact that a couple of orcs were having a conversation nearby wasn't what woke me. All kinds of stuff regularly drifted up through the slats of my loft.

It was the recognition that one of those orcs was Borkul.

I must've honestly thought he'd manage to screw up and fail to deliver Marok's warning, because of the profound relief I felt at hearing his voice in the lodge. He'd even shifted his wiseguy tone for the occasion. Good thing, as I doubted the chieftain would find news of an impending attack a laughing matter.

But as I wondered what Ul-Rott was doing all the way out by the stables, I realized that the other voice wasn't the chieftain's at all. Not unless he was doing a damn good imitation of one of the stable guards.

Specifically, the female stable guard.

"Why did the human wench come to you?" she asked Borkul.

"She feels safe with me. Why else?" As he spoke, I eased off my horse blanket and crept toward the voices. A couple of mules in the stalls below put up a racket—those two were always arguing—which covered the sound of my motions. The far end of the loft overhung the guard quarters. Borkul and the guard were the only ones inside...and they were standing awfully close together.

Not just because they were sharing a secret, either.

He ran a hand down her arm, pausing at the joint of her armor to prod a finger inside in a weirdly intimate gesture. "Don't tell me you're jealous of a human. Even my wife wouldn't care if I coupled with it."

At the mention of his wife, the guard jerked her arm out of his grasp.

Borkul must've known he'd hit a nerve...but unlike the friendly orc I'd traveled through the forest with, he didn't seem to care. "Besides, the human's branded to the house of the blacksmith, and once the dust settles, I'll need him on my side."

"On *our* side," the orc guard said in annoyance.

Borkul took her face in both his hands and pressed his forehead to hers—just like Marok had me. He gentled his voice and repeated, "On *our* side."

With two pairs of tusks, this was about as close as a pair of orcs could get. Which meant, this forehead butt was their equivalent of a kiss. A full-on kiss. On the mouth.

And Marok had done that...to me.

I wasn't a sentimental guy—no one had ever given me any reason to be. But the memory of that closeness I'd shared with Marok—of him cupping my face while we breathed each other's air—squeezed at my jaded heart.

But before I could get too carried away with my silly daydream, the female guard said, "Just so long as the wench hasn't told anyone else. If Ul-Rott's guard is up when Two Swords crosses the river, he might fend them off."

"His defenses will be down. Who would warn him—my *heart-brother*?" Borkul hawked and spat. "Marok's reputation is finished. Even if he said the sky was blue, the chieftain wouldn't take his word for it."

The guard's voice gentled. "It still bothers you. Even though you've made sure he was stripped of all his honor."

"My sister is in the ground while he still lives. The pain of that will never dull."

They butted heads again, but I was no longer interested in their orcish customs of affection. Too busy marveling over the discovery that Borkul wasn't the incompetent lout he pretended to be after all.

He was a traitor.

21

QUINN

The chieftain was in danger, but who could I tell? I doubted Borkul and his mistress were the only traitors, and I had no way of knowing who among Ul-Rott's guard were in league with them.

I was hardly well acquainted with the orcish stronghold, but I did know someone with plenty of his own guards—someone who might be willing to speak to me...if he deemed that the stars had aligned.

I'd have to cross that bridge when I came to it. First, I'd need to get out of the chieftain's lodge.

If I developed a sudden bout of "stomach pain," would the chieftain's guards hustle me off to Taruut's cave, or laugh in my face? It could go either way. Meanwhile, precious minutes would be ticking away.

As if he sensed my indecision, Roy whinnied and gave his

stall a good smack with his dinner-plate hoof. The whole damn barn shook—and I knew what I had to do.

I swallowed hard.

A smarter man would let the damn orcs from across the river go ahead and attack. After all, they'd make a pretty good distraction. But while I might stand a chance at slipping off into the woods once the fighting started, I knew Marok wouldn't join me. Even with his whole clan shunning him, even in disgrace, he would stay and fight for the chieftain who didn't appreciate him. Because that's just who he was.

I climbed down from the loft and crept up to Roy's stall. He whuffed at me, curious what I wanted with him now that our afternoon session was done. Curiosity was good. Horses didn't attack out of curiosity. I pulled a crabapple out of my pocket, opened his stall, and backed toward the exercise yard.

The warhorse followed.

Suddenly I was fiercely aware of my surroundings—the air on my skin, the smell of sodden straw, the distant sound of a smithy's hammer—but mostly the thump of my own heart against my ribs. Roy knew the bridle, and Roy knew me. Whether I'd spook him by slipping that bridle on was anyone's guess.

I dropped the apple. And when he lowered his head to eat it, I made my move.

He'd swallowed the apple in a single gulp and was nosing around for more. While his head was down, I pulled on the bridle in a fluid, decisive motion. If I missed, all bets were off. But I didn't miss—and the bit slid home.

Roy allowed it.

The presence of the bridle would hardly keep him from

flattening me with those hooves—which looked twice as big now from where I was standing. But what it signaled was key: that Roy trusted me.

Hopefully that trust wouldn't get us both killed.

Given the choice, I'd rather use a saddle, but we were out of time. So...bareback, it was. Roy was so tall I had to lead him to the fence to give myself the boost I needed to throw a leg over him. But when I mounted, he didn't so much as flinch—as if I weighed no more than a bored egret hitching a ride. He felt impossibly huge when I straddled him. But my thighs were strong, and I was up for the task.

I'd love to say we vaulted over the fence and set off in a graceful charge—but that would be a lie. Roy was a bright horse, but this was all new to him. I hadn't even been sure my verbal commands had entirely sunk in, but it was a relief to know he'd picked up more than "here's an apple."

We didn't vault the fence, but instead plodded right through, leaving a pile of jagged, splintered planks behind. By the time the guards figured out what was happening, Roy broke into a ball-punishing trot. I pressed harder with my knees and urged him to a canter to outstrip the shouting guards.

By the time we got to the lodge's outer fence, Roy was at a gallop. Big horses like him aren't jumpers—but if I didn't let him have his head, the guards would cut me down without a second thought. Clinging to his mane and bridle for dear life, I clamped down with my knees and squeezed my eyes shut. The ball-thumping motion stopped for a single, soaring moment as we cleared the fence (mostly...there was some splintering wood) and then came down hard on the other side.

I'd been holding on so tight, my hands felt fused to Roy's mane—so tight that trying to unclench my fists would actually hurt. But for now, I focused on steering him toward the shaman's cave without tumbling off his back.

Roy might not be the fastest steed I'd ever ridden, but his stride was long. We reached Taruut before the guards even had time to rally. The old orc was outside, pottering around an herb garden. And while he couldn't see us with his milky jade eyes, he perked up at the sound of Roy's massive hooves pounding the earth, and he lifted up his head—and sniffed.

"Whoa!" I barked—fully prepared for the horse to utterly ignore me. But Roy knew where his apples came from, and he staggered to a clumsy halt and pawed the ground, ribs heaving as he sucked breath from his short gallop across town.

Taruut smiled. "When I threw the ivories, they prophesied something big would happen today...but I never thought it would be this."

I told him about Two Swords' plans—and Borkul's betrayal. And while he had no reason to trust me...for some reason, he did.

"Everything hangs in the balance," he said. "Ul-Rott is hunting south of the village, and someone must warn him. Go. I'll send reinforcements from my honor guard."

I'm not sure if Spear Butt was among the feather-and-paint-studded shamanic guards that escorted me to the gate. I was too busy trying to keep Roy from bucking me off and trampling the orcs who were too close for comfort. Whoever the shaman had sent along, they must've had clout, because the gate guards immediately obeyed them. If orcs respect anything, it's authority. With only a few words, the gate was open, and the road stretched out in front of us.

According to Taruut, the chieftain was hunting in his favorite grove, only an hour's easy walk from the village, so Roy and I should get there fast. But even as I turned down the well-marked path the shaman had described, I realized how easy it would be to nudge Roy down another road. To ride away—and not look back.

The orcish fight over the shifting of a river was not my fight. And the life of a slave was not my life. Yet, although I'd been kicking myself for not taking Silver up on his offer of escape, now that I had yet another opportunity to leave...I gave it only a passing thought, and spurred Roy on to go warn the chieftain.

Orcs can be pretty stealthy when they need to be, but I couldn't say the same for Roy galloping down the forest path. I didn't find the Chieftain's men. They found us—and soon we were surrounded by a good dozen orcs. Ul-Rott didn't go anywhere without his entourage, and Roy and I wouldn't stand a chance against the hunting party. But they'd be no match for a small army.

"Praise Ul-Rott," I said, loud and clear. His guards didn't stand down, exactly, but they did hesitate to spear me off the horse's back and jab me full of holes. "You'll excuse me if I don't kneel. I'm the only thing keeping *Destroyer* from running off."

If not for the horse, I suspect Ul-Rott would have let his men tear me apart. But there I was, astride the warhorse no one could tame. So although he saw me as weak, soft, and overall inferior...when I told him the Two Swords Clan was crossing the river, he listened.

Ul-Rott got his men's attention with a sharp clap, and

announced, "Two Swords sneaks towards us like craven jackals. But we are too clever to fall for their cowardly trap. Back to the village, where we gather our soldiers and fight like real orcs."

Would've been a lot quicker to just say, *Retreat*. But that wasn't the orcish way.

As Roy tore up great hunks of grass and gobbled them down, Ul-Rott rubbed his hands together and sauntered toward us. In a more conversational tone, he added, "And when those sorry excuses for orcs see me on the back of this glorious steed—"

While Ul-Rott rallied his men, one of them took it upon himself to protect Ul-Rott from me—even though I was not only unarmed, but still clinging for dear life to the horse's mane. The guard inserted himself between Ul-Rott and the warhorse. Roy immediately took umbrage to the interruption of his meal, and sent the guy sprawling with a dinner plate hoof to the chest. Somehow I held on, probably because my hands had cramped into a death grip. The guard's chestpiece was caved in and he had the wind knocked out of him. But he'd survive.

In my best diplomatic tone, I said, "Should the mighty Ul-Rott really be seen without a saddle befitting his station?"

It was face-saving bullshit, and we both knew it. But after a moment's consideration, the chieftain gave a curt nod and said, "Of course not. You go ahead to rally the village guard. We march."

None too soon, either. The Two Swords army was not only swelling in numbers, but picking up speed. Luckily, they couldn't move anywhere near as fast as a mounted man.

Roy and I thundered back to the Red Hand Clan. Again,

a branch in the path beckoned—a road that would lead me away to places unknown, but in all likelihood, to a better life than that of an orcish slave. But we charged right past the turn-off. I could have made the excuse that it was Roy returning to what was familiar, not me.

But that, too, was bullshit.

I rounded the final bend, expecting to see the broken gate we'd clumsily tried to vault, and maybe a couple of orcs banging it back together. What I found instead was an army...and at the lead, shoulders squared, head held high, was Marok.

...who Roy very nearly trampled as we skidded to a hasty stop. He was still getting the hang of things.

Strangely enough, when Marok strode up to us, Roy didn't balk like he had with Ul-Rott's personal guard. Maybe because Marok's body language was more confident than aggressive.

Or maybe because Marok smelled like me.

"Ul-Rott is on his way back," I said breathlessly, "But the Two Swords troops are right on his tail."

Marok didn't flinch at the news. Of course he didn't. Taruut had put him back in power for a reason. Whatever disgrace he'd suffered before, it was gone now—he was a general again.

"Orcs don't have tails," Marok said—though he was smiling. Mostly with his eyes. "But we will go and remind them which side of the river is ours."

I was still clutching desperately to the warhorse's mane when Marok reached up and grabbed a fistful of my rough linen shirt. He wasn't trying to haul me off the horse, but rather pull me down to eye-level...so he could press his forehead against mine.

His craggy features blurred as his face filled my aware-ness, but I saw enough to know that his eyes stayed open. My lower lip grazed his through the frame of his tusks, and he gave a small gasp. "Make sure you come back alive," I said, "and we can compare techniques later."

I would've liked to stick around and see Marok off with a jaunty salute, but Roy had other ideas. He'd been worked hard—a lot harder than he was used to—and he was hell-bent on heading back to the stable. Orcs gave us a wide berth as he cantered toward the chieftain's lodge, eager for the familiarity of his stall. The fence around the exercise yard was still in shambles, and he cleared the pile of wood with an easy hop. He was so big, I had to duck down to avoid get-ting brained on the stable's door frame. Thankfully, the side slats of his stall gave me a ladder of sorts to climb down off his back, once I finally worked open my painfully clenched fingers.

We'd shared a big adventure, Roy and me, but I wasn't sure if he'd tolerate a brushing. At the very least, though, I could top off his water trough. I grabbed a bucket and headed for the cistern, walking gingerly. Everything hurt. Back, hips, legs...everything. Dare I suggest Ul-Rott grant me a soak in the sulfur pool to soothe my aching muscles? I was bent over the cistern, deliberating whether I'd get away with asking for a boon, when a shadow fell across the water and blotted out my reflection—the shadow of an orc.

I straightened quickly, expecting one of the chieftain's guards....

But it was Borkul.

And this time, he wasn't smiling.

"Every other slave knows enough to keep their mouth shut and do what they're told. Why ya gotta be so stupid?" An ugly, curved blade flashed in his hand. "Why play the hero?"

I was asking the same question myself—though I suspected I knew the answer. "If I were you," I said, "I'd get out of here while the getting was good, not be wasting time with the likes of me."

He considered the statement, then said, "That's 'cause you think like a pathetic, weak human. Not me—I'm an orc! When someone wrongs me, I punish them. When someone strikes me, I strike back. When someone stops me from taking the revenge I deserve—"

I barely had time to dodge. His knife flashed in a strong arc and sliced open my shirt. I countered with a clumsy swing of the bucket, but it bounced right off Borkul's massive thigh. Water splashed, slicking the dirt into mud. As I scrambled to duck another blow, red blossomed on rough linen, and I realized the shirt wasn't the only thing he'd managed to cut. The blade was so sharp, I couldn't even feel it.

Any of the orcs in the village were capable of killing me, but this was the first one I actually thought would do it. Because now...it was personal.

My foot slipped in the muck and I went down on one knee. Ah, *now* the wound stung. Borkul did smile, then...a smile that chilled me to the bone. All the chieftain's guards had followed Marok out to protect their leader. Anyone left in the village—the kitchen staff, the children, the latrine slave—would hardly get between me and a bloodthirsty warrior.

I dropped all the way down, narrowly avoiding another swing of the sharp blade, then rolled clumsily through the mud to my feet. "Roy, ho!" I yelled, feeling ridiculous even as I called out the words. The horse had made it pretty damn clear he wanted nothing but his stall, but I had to at least try—

With a blood-chilling whinny, Destroyer the orcish war-horse burst from the barn, massive hooves flailing. I balled myself up as small as possible and prepared to be trampled, but Roy knew exactly what he was doing. Hoof met skull with a sickening crunch, and Borkul toppled like a felled oak.

"Easy," I called out, projecting a composure I most surely didn't feel. Roy pranced in place, snorting. But though he was still clearly agitated, he didn't rear up again.

Straightening gingerly, I kicked out and sent Borkul's sharp blade spinning off into the mud, but I needn't have bothered. Rust-red orc blood drooled from his mouth where one of his huge tusks was snapped clean off, and though his eyes were still open, one looked straight ahead while the other lolled to the side. I'd seen head injuries like that before. Orcs might have incredibly robust constitutions, but even so...I doubted he would ever recover.

Roy whinnied and tossed his tangled mane. "Easy," I repeated, and sidled up to give him a pat on the neck. He probably would have preferred a crabapple...but he allowed it.

22

QUINN

Though I did end up recuperating in the shaman's caves, I didn't get my nice hot soak in the sulfur spring, thanks to the big slice across my ribs. It wasn't deep, but Taruut took one whiff of it and declared it would just keep bleeding if he dunked me in the pool. Instead, he parked me on one of his stone slabs and got to work smearing me with his reeking unguents.

Even with nothing more than a hard bed of rock to cushion me, I slept like a baby...thanks to periodic doses of some powerful herbs he'd been cultivating in his garden.

Deep in the humid, sulfurous caves, night and day held no meaning. But it felt as though several days had passed when I woke to the dim light of a nearby brazier, and found Taruut regarding me with his pale, sightless eyes. "You've managed to cause quite a stir," he said with some amusement. "How is it that the ivories did not forewarn me of your coming? Was I too focused on Archibald that my reading was poor? Or is it all interconnected?"

I shrugged, then realized he couldn't see the gesture. "Look, I don't know anything about visions and prophecies. We just all muddle through the best we can."

"Says the man who came through those doors in irons and ended up saving the chieftain's life."

Excitement stirred in my belly. "What are you saying—is Ul-Rott going to free me?"

"You?" He chuckled. "You may have been helpful. But a horse is still a horse, and a slave is still a slave."

I wouldn't have expected any different from the other humans I'd known, so I supposed it was naive to hope for more from an orc.

According to the shaman, the tribe would be gathering in the village square today for a speech—Ul-Rott was big on speeches. And if I was well enough to attend, Taruut would allow it. I was tempted to stay behind, since it was clear the chieftain's gratitude wouldn't grant me my freedom. But given my involvement in stemming off a major attack, I wanted to hear for myself how it all turned out.

My wound was sore and my joints still ached from the wild ride on the biggest horse I'd ever encountered, but I was fine to walk. As I followed Taruut's litter out of the dark humidity of the sulfur caves and into the bright daylight, I noticed Spear Butt giving me the side-eye. But not once did he take a jab at me.

What I didn't notice was a certain traitorous orc anywhere in the recovery chambers. "Did Borkul die?" I asked bluntly, as the shaman seemed pretty tolerant of my questions.

Taruut smiled grimly to himself. "I believe his wife insisted on keeping him alive."

"All things considered, that's awfully, uh, *devoted* of her."

"Devotion has nothing to do with it. His wife should grant him a mercy. But she wants to make sure he suffers with the shame of what he has done for as long as possible."

The whole orc village had turned out for the chieftain's speech, and the guard presence was solid. It was unlikely the Two Swords Clan would be able to rally after the crushing defeat they suffered in the chieftain's hunting grounds, but as I'd learned, orcs take their vengeance very seriously. Best not get too complacent.

Since I was with the shaman's entourage, I had a prime line of sight. The chieftain's guards were decked out in their showiest armor and skull helmets. A group of drummers pounded out an unfaltering rhythm that sharpened the focus of the crowd. And the little ones were in their glory, chowing down on fried lizards on sticks—then jabbing each other when the sticks were stripped clean.

Once the crowd was whipped into an expectant frenzy, Ul-Rott swaggered to the dais in the center and held up a massive hand. The crowd fell silent. Even the younglings who were giddy with lizard.

"Let all bear witness to our victory," the chieftain proclaimed in a booming voice. "Not only has the Two Swords Clan been driven off, fleeing like hunted rabbits, but a turncoat has been routed from our clan. Cast Borkul's name from your tongue. He exists no more."

As one, the crowd answered with a mighty, hacking bark—a sound I don't think I'd even be able to produce, not without a good amount of practice. It was clearly pretty cathartic. Everyone seemed satisfied that excluding Borkul from the clan was the worst punishment he could receive.

"And for exemplary service," Ul-Rott went on, "A boon has been earned by someone all of you have underestimated..."

My heart thrummed harder than the deep kettle drums as I wondered if maybe Taruut was wrong about my freedom after all.

"...my staunch and determined commander, General Marok."

Of course, I wanted my freedom. And I might have been the one who'd tamed the untamable warhorse and galloped out to warn everyone...but was I disappointed to see Marok regain the respect he'd lost?

Not even a little.

Marok had always looked big and solid to me. But with the mantle of honor resting on his broad shoulders, he seemed positively massive. It wasn't pride he radiated, either, but dignity. The knowledge that bravery and integrity would ultimately triumph.

My jaded heart begged to differ...but I couldn't deny that in his true element, Marok was not just formidable, but magnificent.

He strode to center stage and folded fluidly to one knee. "Praise Ul-Rott."

The chieftain enjoyed his subjugation for just a moment, then said, "Stand, warrior. And claim your prize."

Without so much as a moment of hesitation, Marok swung an arm around to point unerringly at me, and said, "I will have the human slave."

Ul-Rott's craggy brow furrowed. "But your former heart-brother still lives. He who betrayed you."

"The human," Marok repeated.

Ul-Rott glanced at me, absently toying with one of his iron-shod tusks, then turned his attention back to Marok. "You have served me well, there's no doubt. But my steed needs its trainer. Besides, you have no horse, no stable. Just take the traitor's head and be pleased with it."

"I don't want the human for my stable. I want him for my bed."

A murmur rippled through the crowd...and not just because orcs didn't technically *have* beds, either. But it was nowhere near the uproar this announcement would have garnered in the Fortifications—where, frankly, I couldn't picture anyone publicly saying such a thing at all.

Even the chieftain seemed surprised, though only mildly so. "Well, then. What do I care where the human sleeps? He must report daily to the stables. But if you want him in your household, this I shall grant." He stroked his tusk. "Though I, personally, would have preferred the head."

23

QUINN

When orcs celebrate, they don't hold back. And in driving off their enemies, the Red Hand Clan had plenty of reason for celebration. But for all that Marok had longed for his kinsmen to acknowledge him again, he was eager to leave the festivities. And so was I. As soon as the chieftain stepped down from the dais, we went back to Marok's dwelling. Taking in that tidy timber-built home crammed with all his trophies and spoils, I felt less like a stranger in a strange land, and more like a wanderer who'd finally found his way home.

I'd last crossed the threshold to Marok's house as a slave. And now?

Well, I guess I was still a slave.

"They say Borkul wounded you," Marok said. "I can always petition the chieftain for your revenge—"

"No head." I gestured toward his packed shelves. "Where

on earth would we keep it?"

Marok considered me. "Your words are light...but a man's scent never lies."

He could *smell* my trepidation? That would take some getting used to.

He removed his heavy chest-plate and hung it from a stout rack. "I thought you would prefer living here to the stable," he said. "But if I'm wrong, and—"

"That's not it." With nowhere to sit and legs far too sore to squat, I settled for leaning against the wall. "Don't get me wrong. This is a fine house—lack of furniture notwithstanding. And the prospect of being with you—"

My scent must have shifted when I recalled how hot it had been to ride his muscular thigh. He whiffed the air, and I felt myself blush like a stable boy stumbling across the red lantern district for the first time.

"Anyway, the point is, I want to be here because I choose to be. Not because you own me. I don't expect you to understand. Our people are too different. You're an orc, and you have a certain way of seeing things, and in your eyes, I'm just some lowly human—"

Marok was fast for his size—stunningly quick—and he flattened me against the wall before I even had a chance to blink. He pressed his broad face into my hair, framing my skull with his tusks, and *breathed* me, filling my senses with his rock-hard muscles, his mossy earthen scent, and his overwhelming presence. His voice was a low rumble that vibrated my whole body when he said, "You're wrong, Quinn. There's nothing lowly about you. The orc soldiers are twice bigger than you, but you never cringe or quail. All of them are terrified of the warhorse—and only you were brave enough to earn its trust. But most important of all, where I failed to warn Ul-Rott of the attack, you made him listen. I don't see you as a human...but as a hero."

Back in the Fortifications, I'd been plenty of things. An ambitious dreamer. A clever horseman. Even a good lay.

But I'd never been anybody's hero.

I flexed my hips and found myself straddling that muscular thigh again. And just like a horse that's finally grasped its training, my body shifted from caution to arousal so fast it left my head spinning. Marok was so phenomenally big I could hardly make sense of him all. And he'd called me a *hero*.

His bulk wasn't intimidating—it was fucking sexy. And when I slid my arms around his waist, he didn't try to shrug me off. No...he pressed closer.

He was so huge, I had to strain to reach my arms all the way around him. The thought of doing the same with my legs made my pulse throb low in my groin.

And Marok knew it.

"I've never lain with a human before," he said into my hair. "Tell me what pleases you."

All this big, solid hotness...*and* he was a giver?

Damn.

"Touch me," I said as I slid my hands down to clutch the muscular globes of his ass. "Everywhere. Not just my dick. Run your whiskers down my neck. And if you don't mind the taste of human—"

Marok grunted and spun me toward the center of the room. He grabbed a pelt from the cabinet, the bottom of the stack, and the whole pile slid to the floor in a haphazard heap. If it weren't for my wound, I suspected he would have just shoved me right down on top of them. But he restrained himself—tense all over, nostrils flaring, chest heaving.

He pulled off his gauntlets and said, "Goblins don't take off their tabards. And ogres only fuck things from behind so they're harder to stab. But humans...?"

I shucked off my clumsy linen shirt. "Naked is good. Naked is very good. And as for any stabbing —well, that remains to be seen." I would definitely get off on him impaling me—over and over—till I forgot my own name. I just wasn't sure it was physically possible. Because the "weapon" in question was straining against Marok's leather breeches now, trapped against one leg. And it was just as massive as everything else on him.

He stripped bare to the waist and pressed me down onto the mound of thick, luxurious furs. They slid into place all around us, softer than the choicest featherbed. Marok did touch me then—only to ghost his fingers over the slash I'd taken across the ribs. "I should give you more time to heal—"

I grabbed his hand and brought it to my mouth, grazing my lips over his hard, callused palm. His pupils dilated. "If we don't do this here and now, Marok, I might just explode. Are you sure you want that on your conscience?"

"You and your questions," he said...and yanked down my breeches.

My hard cock sprang free and lay heavy against my treasure trail. At the sight of it, Marok made a bestial grunt, deep in his throat—then immediately dove down and rubbed his face all over it. I froze, suddenly hyperaware of his tusks sliding along my pelvis. The cool ivory was a stark contrast both to the heat of his breath, and to the tickle of the fine, downy, green hairs that furred his upper lip.

He must have liked what he smelled, because he pressed in deep to the crease of my thigh, snuffling against my balls in a way that made me squirm and gasp. It would have been ticklish, if not for the weight of his rock-hard body flattening me into the furs. Soft and hard. Hot and cold. Everything lighting up my senses, all at once.

And when the wetness of his tongue glided over my taint, I nearly bent myself double arching up off the furs.

Marok's head jerked up and he made a curious grunt, and I hastened to add, "That's good. Really good."

His tusks framed a shadow of a smile as he pressed his face back down between my legs and proceeded to utterly undo me. His tongue was smooth and hot and deliciously wet. Notably muscular, too, as it prodded into me with relentless insistence.

I grabbed my aching dick and Marok shoved my hand away. I might not want to be owned—but the feeling of him working me over with his tongue and his breath and his big, hard hands had me inching toward the point of not caring about anything but the beckoning peak.

And then all sensation stopped as he eased back on his knees to take a look at me. Maybe the ogres were onto something about doing it from behind. With my breeches around my ankles and my knees splayed open, I felt incredibly naked and exposed. My hair was tangled in the furs and my cheeks burned hot. It was a far cry from a quick tug in the alley behind a Fortifications saloon.

"Your ass likes my tongue." No one had ever claimed something so bold—and a thrill coursed through me as Marok unlaced his breeches one-handed, slowly stroking my dick, drawing out the pleasure, not seeking its end. I liked this new, confident Marok. "Humans and orcs aren't so different after all."

His breeches opened and his cock fell free. I'd expected it to match his pale, greenish skin, but it wasn't entirely green. The dark orcish blood engorging the veins mottled it with a webwork of brown, like some exotic plant.

Some very *large* exotic plant.

"I wish I could take that," I said. "But you're just too damn big."

But before I could offer him a hand-job, he grabbed a stoppered bottle from a nearby shelf and said, "There's a way."

That orcish dick was as thick around as my wrist. "As hot as it might be—no way is it going to fit."

"Not on its own," he said, as if that fact couldn't be more obvious. He pried out the cork with his teeth and spat it out. It bounced off the wall and rolled away. "That's what this is for. Easewater. Night laurel to relax you. Rocknut oil to slick the way. And dreamweed to dull the pain."

I swallowed hard. I'm no herbalist and had no clue about the first two things, though I'd seen the dreamweed at work on the blade of the goblin's knife. Potent stuff, no doubt. But the sheer size of him—

"I might not have coupled with a human, but I know orcs who have. With this." He brandished the herbal mixture.

"And the human lived to tell about it? Remember...I'm gonna need to get on a horse in the near future—"

"Quinn," he said calmly. "I would never hurt you." He seemed so sure. "Do you trust me?"

Despite the sheer enormity of his dick...I did. I glanced at the thick, veined shaft, steeled myself, and nodded.

He decanted a slick of glistening potion on his finger...then nudged it into the crack of my buttocks.

Even his blunt, hard finger might've been more well-endowed than a few of my more disappointing tavern encounters, and the feel of it breaching my ass, slippery with fragrant oil, sent a fresh surge of want rushing down toward my groin.

Marok scented the air, looking well-pleased with himself—and I guessed he wasn't sniffing the easewater. That look was almost enough to make me regret that the numbing dreamweed wouldn't let me feel much of anything. So long as he didn't get it on my dick, though, no doubt that elusive peak would beckon to me again soon.

Marok took his time greasing me up, dipping into the bottle again and again. Not just readying me, but probing deep with his thick finger, teasing me, learning just where his touch would make me gasp. Watching my face. Learning my body. I was used to quick gropes and stolen moments. Not this unyielding scrutiny. He was just as methodical with my ass as he was with everything else, and soon my dick was impossibly hard, leaking its own slickness against my belly.

Though when he climbed up over me and set his weight on his elbows, blotting out my awareness of everything but him, the solid prod at my body's entrance was still daunting. "I thought you said I'd be numb from the dreamweed."

"No, I said it would take away the pain." Marok angled himself thoughtfully and flexed his hips. "Why bother coupling if you don't feel it?" A push. Resistance. Too much—too big. He grabbed a handful of my hair to anchor himself and pressed again. But it would never—

A guttural moan escaped me as his tapered cockhead forced past the resistance and breached my slickened hole.

Marok echoed the sound with a deep rumble.

With excruciating care, he backed out a few inches...then pressed in again, even harder.

This. This. This.

I'd been starving for something deeper and I hadn't even realized it. Not until an orc was filling me with his impossibly big dick.

I wrapped my legs around him and my hip joints throbbed. My wild ride on Destroyer's back was nothing compared to what Marok was doing to me now. Everywhere we brushed together, some novel sensation reminded me the man between my legs was no human. The pebbly hardness of his hide skimming my inner thighs. His tusk gliding along my temple. The downy fur of his upper lip teasing my forehead. The forest-floor scent of him blossoming between us as we both began to sweat and strain.

It was the slowest, most deliberate fuck I'd ever had—that I ever could have even imagined. Inch by painstaking inch, Marok worked his way in. Spreading me. Filling me.

Undoing me.

There was no pain, but the pressure was nothing short of exquisite. I climbed as I was filled and filled and filled, my heartbeat throbbing in my engorged cock leaking slickness all over my belly. I felt like I could hang there on the cusp of my orgasm forever...until Marok slipped a hand between us and wrapped his callused palm around my weeping dick.

I didn't just come. I came apart.

Even in my throes of pleasure, I knew Marok was struggling to control himself. He couldn't push all the way in—not without disemboweling me. I'd taken maybe a third of him, at best. But that must've been enough.

His orgasm followed right on the heels of mine. He grunted and went rigid all over, and soon the slipperiness of the sex oil morphed into something else entirely as he pumped me full of his wet, hot seed.

Even spent, he stayed there between my legs, gazing down at me with a look I wasn't sure I could interpret. Possibly... tender? Though between the green skin and the tusks, it was kind of hard to tell. "You and I are much alike," he said.

The opposite of what I was thinking...but I kept my mouth shut and waited for him to explain. Marok could be a real cipher, and I was curious to know what was going on behind that staid exterior.

He gave his words a moment's consideration, then said, "I am a warrior. I could never be a slave. And you are just as proud."

Well...he wasn't wrong.

As if to bring home his point, Marok rolled us into the furs so he was no longer over me, but side by side—as an equal. "Anyone in the Red Hand Clan is either an orc or a slave. There's no room here for anything in between—this isn't the bazaar with its mix of races. But claiming you for this household means that any orc who wrongs you would answer to me."

"It's for my own protection. I get it." Though my tone may have said otherwise.

"I have claimed you in front of the chieftain and the clan—and you are mine. But...." Marok reached tentatively for my hair, seemed to think better of it...then changed his mind again and ran his fingers through the strands as if he'd never touched anything quite like it. "If you wish to leave, I will escort you from our territory myself."

I noted he didn't say he'd come with me. Maybe that was a promise he simply couldn't make.

The men I'd spent time with back in the Fortifications would promise me the stars and the moon—but once they got off, I'd be lucky if they bought me a drink. I realized I liked it a lot better when promises actually meant something.

"So...I need to get my face branded?"

Marok gave an orcish huff. "Not with my scent all over you."

Well. We'd need to make sure we rubbed ourselves together on a regular basis. No great hardship there.

Marok's fondling of my hair emboldened me to skim my fingertips over the craggy ridge of his brow, then trail them along the smooth hardness of his tusks. "We have an expression where I come from, to seal it with a kiss. I'm guessing that's not really a thing here."

"It's not." He trailed a finger down my cheekbone. "But if you wish to show me how it goes, I will learn."

Speaking of the Fortifications, I couldn't help but think back to my last fateful encounter with the blacksmith's apprentice—the one that had inspired me to seek greener pastures, and eventually landed me here. I'd gone in for something more intimate than our usual hand-jobs...and it hadn't ended well. As little as this felt like my final tryst with that big oaf, as I eased myself up and pressed my face to Marok's, my body viscerally recalled the moment I'd been shoved away. But Marok didn't balk. He was very still. And when I carefully fit my face between his tusks and skimmed my tongue across his lower lip, he gave a low murmur of satisfaction.

His downy upper lip tickled my stubble as he opened to

my kiss. And I decided I could live with the other orcs calling me a slave—just as long as here, where it counted, this proud orc general and I were truly equals.

24

ARCHIE

I really should've been dead.

The brazier's fire had dwindled and the humid cave air was wet in my lungs...but somehow, I found myself taking a deeper breath than I had in ages. It surprised me. Once the illness settled in, I must've well and truly thought I'd never get better.

And why should I? I'd burned through so many lives already, it was ridiculous to think I would get another chance. I'd been born with my cord wrapped around my neck, blue as a sapphire and still as a stone. But somehow the midwife managed to slap some life into me. She couldn't do the same for my mum—but honestly, what can you expect from a two-bit leech?

Maybe death didn't want me. I'd survived being passed around a group of marauders and left for dead, and even made it through the slaver's tent with my hide intact. Maybe I truly would recover. I took another experimental breath. Yep. Breathing was indeed getting easier.

I swung down off the stone slab I'd affectionately dubbed my *bier* and set off in search of Taruut. The shaman spent all his waking hours plying me with incantations and herbs, so he'd be thrilled to finally see me up and around. *You're the key to everything,* he'd always be telling me—and while his whole mystic routine was clearly just a bunch of mumbo-jumbo to keep his clan happy, I'd grown pretty fond of the weird old guy.

Unfortunately, I couldn't say the same for his lackeys. If I knew anything at all, I knew men. And while these might be a lot bigger and a little greener than the sort I normally dealt with in the brothels, their macho swagger was the same. The important thing was to show no fear. Men like that got off on lording their power over others. When you proved to them that you didn't really give a damn, you spoiled all their fun and they would leave you alone.

Unless they smacked you into next week—I touched the healing handprint on my cheek—but usually they left you alone.

I followed a dim passage, reflecting on the fact that I had no idea where I was going because up until now, I wasn't able to walk. My legs were still shaky and I definitely needed to put away something more substantial than the herbal broth I'd been subsisting on, but at least I was upright.

Sound carried funny in the caves, where plinks and plunks of water echoed like bells, and the hiss of steam occasionally spat from a random fissure. I came upon a chamber brimming with weird mushrooms and another filled with bones. And somehow, I'd managed to go in a full circle and end up right where I'd started. Either that or there were just an awful lot of skulls around. Soon, I was exhausted from my wandering and fatigued by the weight of the lantern. But when I doubled back to slip onto my trusty bier, I found myself instead in a tunnel that ended in a tapestry. A pretty gruesome one, rife with images of orcs beheading things.

I was peering at the workmanship on a spurting spine when I realized the tapestry was gently shifting. I poked at the beheaded creature, and the fabric moved. It wasn't covering a wall—but a passageway.

I lifted a corner of the weighty tapestry and slipped past. The room beyond was dark and close, filled with all kinds of juju nonsense, all of it thick with the smell of orc. I held up my lantern to get my bearings, and a mound of cloth in the corner stirred. Startled, I blundered into a pile of painted bones, and they clattered almost musically to the stone floor.

The cloth shifted, and then said on a ragged breath, "Archibald...."

"Taruut?" I hurried over and folded to my knees, thinking the old man must have fallen—or worse, that some rival had slipped past his guards and attacked him. But, no, he was just lying there on the ground with an embroidered coverlet pulled up to his neck.

Or maybe...it was a shroud.

"Do you need help?" I said, all in a rush. "Are you hurt?"

He beckoned for me to come closer, and I bent my ear to his lips. Up close, I realized his breathing had the same wet rattle to it that mine did—and even in the dark, stifling heat of the cave, my blood ran cold.

While the old man had been curing me, I hadn't just been

lying around doing nothing. I'd been hard at work contaminating him.

"Where's that bitter soup you've been pouring down my gullet? I'll go get some—it'll put you right in no time."

I'd meant to scramble to my feet—to do something, anything, to make myself useful. But Taruut's gnarled hand shot out from under the fabric and clamped around my wrist like irons.

"It's fitting that you're here." His voice was a hollow wheeze. Barely a breath. "Bear witness to the event that will bring an end to the conflict with our neighbors once and for all."

"Oh?" I said with forced brightness. "And what's that?"

But instead of an answer, the blind shaman just smiled a cryptic smile as his hand fell from my wrist, and with a final wheeze, he went silent.

About This Book

I played a lot of D&D when I was younger, so I was pretty darned excited when orc romance emerged as a mini-genre of its own. I don't think I ever played an orc as anything more than a bad guy to be mowed down—so it was really fun to get into the orcish culture and mindset, and then to switch points of view between Quinn and Marok to show how they see each other versus how they see themselves.

When Quinn first meets Marok, all he sees are their differences. Human and orc. Captive and master. Refined and rugged. Their worlds couldn't be further apart.

Or so it seems.

What drew me to write their story wasn't just the tension of opposites attracting—though there's certainly a pull between them right from the start. It was the revelation waiting beneath the surface: these two men, despite everything that divides them, share a profound similarity that neither initially recognizes.

Both know what it means to be ostracized.

Quinn's fall from grace in the noble houses left him vulnerable to the very slavers who delivered him to orc territory. One indiscretion made public, and the doors that once opened for him slammed shut. Meanwhile, Marok had been dealing with not only his own grief, but the weight of silent judgment following his every move. This shared experience of rejection creates the unexpected bridge between them.

I've always believed the most interesting romances happen not just when characters are drawn to their differences, but when they recognize themselves in the other—often in ways they never expected.

This interplay of similarity and difference forms the beating heart of their story. The initial friction—captive versus captor, civilized versus savage (or so each culture would claim)—gradually reveals itself as the perfect foundation for deeper understanding. Their contrasting approaches to the world don't divide them—they offer new perspectives, new solutions, new possibilities neither would have discovered alone.

It was a journey for Quinn and Marok to even see each other as people, and that was fun to write. I loved watching them share experiences that eventually bound them together to build something stronger than either could have created alone.

That's the romance I wanted to capture. Not just the heat of attraction across boundaries, but the profound recognition that can happen when two people who thought they couldn't be more different discover how deeply they understand each other.

If you enjoy Quinn and Marok's story, please consider leaving a review. As this represents a new direction for my writing, your feedback helps tremendously and encourages other readers to discover this world I'm so excited to share.

MASTER STROKE

Bonus Short

MAROK

The smell of tanned hide was so thick you could almost take the air itself for leather. Ever since news of Ul-Rott's warhorse got out, the common square of the Red Hand Clan reeked of tannin, saddle soap, and the desperate hope of merchants. A half-dozen leather workers had descended on the village, each more eager than the last.

And while Destroyer was big, he could only wear so much tack. But since there were more tanners in the square than I'd normally see in a year, I decided I might as well make use of them.

An unmanned stall filled with leather work caught my eye, mainly because most merchants guard their property with their lives, even in an orcish village where everyone knows better than to steal. But then I saw the stall hadn't been abandoned after all. A leathery figure emerged from amongst the wares, revealing a gnome as brown and creased as the merchandise he sold.

His finely stitched leather cap was slightly askew, pulled down tight over his head. He was a wiry creature, spindly even for a gnome, with long fingers stained black with tannin. They moved like nimble spiders over his wares as he sized me up.

I didn't normally bother with gnomes. Too clever by half for their own good—at least in their own minds. I turned my eyes to one of the many belts on display.

"That's the finest leather from the great gray mountain elk," claimed the gnome. I highly doubted it. More likely it was common deer hide, but the tanning was so fresh, I smelled nothing but oak bark and tallow. The gnome flicked his cunning gaze over me, noting everywhere a gemstone glinted from my things. A general's bloodthirsty rubies at my throat. A keen tiger's eye at my belt—a gift from Akala. And a fire quartz at my pommel to add strength to my blows.

Then he noted my boots. Custom, of course. But sturdy and well fitted. Clearly expensive.

"The *finest* leather," he repeated.

I supposed his workmanship looked decent enough.

The gnome grabbed an elaborately tooled knife sheath from the display. The most ostentatious sheath, I saw. "If the belt doesn't suit your taste, how about this sturdy holder?" he pressed, flexing the leather. "It'll keep your blade sharp and close."

My current knife sheath served me well. I didn't need another. In fact, I didn't need anything. I only bought the best, and I took good care of my possessions.

But the same couldn't be said for Quinn, who'd so recently lost everything. And while he was welcome to any possession under the roof we shared, many of my things were ungainly in his nimble hands.

Even as I pictured his slender, sure fingers, my gaze fell on the coils of a light leather whip. At the stables, Quinn had an array of such tools at his disposal, but he found them all clumsy and thick. And while he seldom complained, he did once mention a whip lost to the slavers. He'd been quick to add he was better off now, anyhow. But I'd noted the edge of wistfulness in his voice.

I nodded toward the whip. "How much?"

Calculations danced in the merchant's eyes. I prepared to haggle—as unbefitting as the practice might be for a warrior—but the gnome surprised me by saying, "You don't want *that* whip. It's far too small to do you any good."

"It's for a human."

"Ahhh...." The gnome's bushy eyebrows rose until they were lost beneath his overworked leather cap. "I see. I see. Well, that's fine, then. For you? Just three coppers."

I was already eager to be done with the conversation. He must have been expecting me to bargain, and grew alarmed when I didn't. As I pulled out my purse, he hastened to add, "And as an added bonus, I'll throw in a pot of honeyed lanolin."

I scowled at the whip. "Is the leather not properly conditioned?"

"All of my wares are tanned and tooled with the utmost care," he huffed. "I'd never sell shoddy workmanship. The salve is for your human."

Who had access to all the same provisions I did. I narrowed my eyes.

The gnome must have thought I was dense, because his tone was patronizing when he added, "You're its master—don't you know? Their skin is ridiculously fragile."

At the thought of the pristine expanse of Quinn's back marred by raised red welts, a crimson haze descended, and the metallic tang of bloodlust spread across my tongue.

The gnome rambled on. "Humans are like butterflies. Nice

to look at. But grab it from the air and its delicate beauty crumbles in your hand."

Muscles coiled and tendons strained as every fiber braced to unleash devastation upon any who threatened what was mine. But there was no enemy before me—no one daring to harm Quinn. Just a wrinkled brown gnome with a look of confusion on his face. He glanced down at my arm showing just above my bracers—its skin pebbled with anger—then shrugged and said, "Well, at least if your human takes it in its mind to turn that whip on you, I doubt you'll even feel a thing."

I shoved my coins into his hand, grabbed the whip from the display, and strode back to my house with protective anger smoldering in my belly. Useless anger, because there was no threat. And still, the mere idea of anyone touching Quinn—my Quinn—filled me with rage.

Leather squeaked as my hand tightened around the whip. I should never have purchased the thing. If Quinn thought, for even a moment, that I would ever strike him....

When I shoved through my front door, Quinn stood in the common room, assessing the wooden bench he'd commissioned, one of many new pieces. He turned neatly, shifted his weight, and looked me up and down. His hair tumbled to his shoulders, glossy and black as a raven's wing, and the corner of his soft mouth curved in a half-smile. So graceful. So *delicate*. And yet, I scented not a trace of fear.

He quirked an eyebrow. "I know that look, Marok. What's got your hackles up?"

"It's nothing."

"Is that so?" Quinn stood between me and all the new "furniture" he claimed we needed. Even with the various new surfaces crowding the room, there was nowhere for me to tuck away the whip before he saw it, and his shrewd eyes went immediately to the braided coil of leather in my hands. "And what have we here?"

Flustered, I stammered, "It was...I simply thought...I would never—"

But Quinn had already snatched the whip from my unresisting fingers. He pulled the coil taut between two hands with a small snap, then took an easy step back as the loop of leather unfurled.

"Not in the house!" I blurted—but I was too late.

When he reared back, the movement was so economical, so subtle, it was hardly a gesture at all. His lean body drew itself into perfect, deadly lines that made my breath catch, and I stood helpless at the sight of him. But then the whip sang through the air, and the pin of my bearskin cloak clattered to the floorboards before I could even flinch. The heavy fur pooled at my feet as Quinn looked on with a grin of satisfaction. And despite all the things around us, not so much as a dust mote had been disturbed.

"It'll do," he said teasingly—then closed the distance between us and pressed his lithe body up against mine. The fingers of his free hand tangled possessively in my hair as he drew me down into a kiss.

His mouth was as sure as his hands. His tongue parted my lips. Bold—insistent. And as he claimed me with his kiss, the scent of his heady human arousal blossomed around us. Kissing might be a human thing, but it made heat rush straight to my groin. Soon, my own musk mingled with his.

Our scents blended well.

Against my lips, where I couldn't quite meet his eyes,

Quinn murmured, "Of all the things I lost when the slavers took me—my whip was the one thing I thought was irreplaceable. Who would've guessed that I'd end up with something even better?"

"It is sturdy gnomish craftsmanship," I allowed.

A huff of a laugh played across my damp lower lip. "That's not why it's so perfect. Not at all."

Quinn let go of the whip and it slithered to the floor, nesting in my cloak like a serpent. He needed the free hand to unhitch my belt. It dropped down beside my pin. Then, with a movement just as graceful as his whip strike, he folded to his knees. Another tug, and I was hobbled by my leather breeches. I buried my fingers in his raven hair—sleek as silk—but then checked my strength. My thoughts had turned to crushed bits of butterfly wings.

But Quinn grabbed my thickening cock by the root, shoved it up toward my belly, and whispered against my balls, "Stop holding back. I can take it."

Our gazes locked. His eyes danced with challenge—an expression entirely unbefitting a human slave. And entirely Quinn.

When I made a fist of his hair, the musk of his wanting filled my nostrils. He purred low in his throat as I shoved my cockhead into his eager mouth.

The wet heat was sublime. The inside of a human's mouth must be made for sucking cocks. Everything was smooth and slick and perfect. He could hardly fit more than the tip, but that was the most sensitive part. And he worked my shaft with both hands while he sucked it.

I clenched his hair harder and he hummed his approval. His resilience, his audacity, his sheer will to survive and thrive—it was intoxicating. I tried to hold back, but the sensations were too intense—and just like the whip, Quinn knew how to wield them with exacting precision. The room was filled by the mingling of our scent as I plundered his mouth. I didn't last long. I couldn't. Quinn forced my surrender, and I was undone. I locked my knees and thrust with abandon, and while Quinn faltered, he quickly regained his balance and finished me.

With a deep sigh of contentment, I opened my eyes. Quinn still knelt at my feet, staring back up at me as I traced his fine cheekbone with my knuckle. My spunk webbed his silken hair—whatever spend he hadn't managed to swallow—and his lips were flushed and ripe. But what captivated me most of all was the look of self-satisfaction that gleamed in his sharp eyes. He might not be as strong as me...but he knew exactly how to get under my skin.

Quinn was no fragile butterfly. He was a wasp.

www.ingramcontent.com/pod-product-compliance
Lightning Source LLC
Chambersburg PA
CBHW020120180626
46812CB00006B/2672